Their Makeshift Marriage

LEIGH MICHAELS

PBL Limited
Ottumwa Iowa

Copyright 2021 Leigh Michaels

ISBN 13: 978-1-892689-84-9

Printed in the United States of America

This is a work of fiction. Characters and events portrayed in this book have no existence outside the imagination of the author. Any resemblance to real persons, living or dead, or real events is purely coincidental.

For all the readers
who have waited patiently
for this book:
Thank you!

Chapter One

Of course, the house was the biggest one in the most elite neighborhood in Mayfair. Five windows marched in precise lines across each of the upper levels, and on the ground floor, four even larger ones – two on each side of a shiny black door – looked out over the park which lay at the center of Grosvenor Square. Through the panes of glass, Thea saw swatches of ornate lace, heavy brocade, and brightly-colored velvet, forming a rainbow cascading down the six levels of the facade.

Clearly the owner of this establishment didn't fret about the tax levied on every window in London.

Beside Thea, the maid whispered, "I never been inside a place that fancy, miss."

Neither have I.

Thea steadied her wobbly knees. "It's only a house, Alice. And it's just people living there. Regular people." Maybe if she said it loudly enough, she'd believe it herself – but obviously Alice was no more convinced than Thea was. "Anyway, you're not going in. You'll wait for me here at the edge of the park, as we discussed."

Alice nodded agreeably. "So if you get taken prisoner by the slavers and shipped off to Algeria to a harem, I can at least tell Madame what happened to you."

No point in telling Alice again how unlikely it was that any such thing could happen right in the middle of Mayfair... even if explaining would let her delay a little longer and consider whether she really wanted to do this.

Thea straightened her shoulders. She had to go ahead. The house – with its general air of affluence – confirmed that the man who owned it could well afford to pay what he owed. It would be a pittance to him, even though it was a fortune to her. Surely all she need do was state the facts and tell him that if he paid his debt, she would remain silent. But if he *didn't* pay...

Shadows fell across the front door, which was recessed a couple of feet, and it wasn't until Thea stood on the top step that she saw the black wreath around the knocker – the black wreath that said the house had recently experienced a death.

She froze. Was she too late? Was the wreath a memorial for the man she had come to see?

And if it was, what would she do?

* * *

Will stood on the Axminster carpet in front of the earl's paper-strewn desk, feeling as though he had been called to the headmaster's office to be scolded. The only difference, he supposed, was that he was too big these days for a caning – though it would have been obvious to a blind man that Carrington would have liked to do just that.

His lordship pushed his chair back from the desk. "Six months," he growled. "You've had six months. And the best you can do is to say, *The trail is cold*?" His voice rose in a weird falsetto.

Will hoped to hell he didn't really sound like that when he made his reports to clients. "Yes, sir," he said steadily. *Though it's more like there's no trail at all.* "It would help a great deal in the search if you would tell me why you want to find this woman, or how long ago it is that you lost track of her, or how you came to know her..." He spotted the red gleam in Carrington's eyes and paused. Opera dancer, he'd wager. Or perhaps actress. No wonder Carrington didn't want to admit the nature of the relationship.

But why his lordship was looking for this woman, and why he was unwilling to part with any other information than a name... that was more than Will could guess. "I'm a solicitor, sir, not a Bow Street Runner. Perhaps you should—"

"*One* task," Carrington growled. "One simple task, and it's more than you can handle. You should be groveling in shame, yet here you stand as though it's *my* fault you can't carry out a simple task."

Nobody ever said Carrington played fair. But if he expected Will to grovel – hell, no. "If you have nothing new to add to my instructions, I'll say good morning to you, sir." Will pivoted and strode toward the door.

"Some peer you'd be." Carrington's voice whipped across the room, and despite himself Will felt the sting turning his neck red.

"I never asked for the job, sir." As soon as the words were out, he regretted them. Letting Carrington goad him never accomplished anything.

And despite his irritation, he felt a whisper of sympathy for the man at the desk. Carrington hadn't expected his only son to die. Of course he wasn't pleased that Will suddenly stood in Robert's place as the next heir to the earldom. Will was only a distant cousin, a man who in Carrington's view was not fit for the role because he earned his bread taking instructions from others and carrying out their wishes.

"And you'd better not expect it now, either. Not if there's anything I can do about it."

Carrington's words were so quiet Will almost didn't catch them, but he turned, one hand on the doorknob. "Sir?"

"Nothing. Never mind. Just – find that woman!"

Will sighed and strode out into the hall, wishing that he dared slam the door behind him.

Find Anna Winslow. With no description, no time frame, no age, no family connection to go on. With no hint of where or when Anna Winslow might have crossed paths with the Earl of Carrington.

Last year? A decade ago? As much as half a century? – the man was pushing sixty. Will hadn't thought to go that far back; he'd assumed – knowing what he did about Carrington – that she had been a paramour. But perhaps he was wrong and Anna Winslow had been an acquaintance from Carrington's boyhood, someone he had known at the family seat in Hampshire. Should he make a trip out to Monkscroft and ask questions there?

An odd comment, that, about the title. *You'd better not expect it—not if I can do anything about it*. But what could

Carrington possibly do? Unless…

For the first time, Will considered the question of Anna Winslow in a different light. What if she had been associated with Robert rather than with his lordship?

He was lost in thought as he crossed the dim entry hall toward the front door, and only a hint of motion at the base of the stairs caught his attention. *Just when you think things can't get worse…*

He made his bow. "Good morning, Lady Carrington."

A tall, gaunt, sharp-edged woman, dressed in unrelieved black, swung around to face him, her eyes bleak. "It is hardly that, Mr. Archer. There are no good mornings since my son died. I see you've at least stopped wearing that black armband. What a mark of hypocrisy it was for you to try to convince the world you're sorry to have suddenly stepped into his shoes!" She stormed up the stairs.

Brilliant. Just another day at the Carringtons' London home.

Wearily, Will nodded at the footman who held out his hat and walking stick. "Thank you, Jenkins."

The footman allowed a small, sympathetic smile to pass across his face as he opened the door, but he was too well-trained – or too fearful of consequences – to speak.

The hinges creaked as the door swung wide, and a woman standing just outside spun around to face him. Will rushed to clutch her arm as she stepped backward off the top stair, flailing for balance. He tugged her to safety on the stoop. Her silky cloak swirled around her, releasing the soft aroma of some slightly-spicy flower, one he ought to be able to identify. One he no doubt would have recognized had he grown up in the country, on the Carrington estate, rather than with the sea and shipping smells of Southampton.

She looked pointedly down at his hand, still clamped on her arm.

Stop thinking about flowers. Will felt a strange reluctance to let go, but he released her arm and stepped back. "I hope I didn't bruise you, Miss."

"Even if that's the case, it is nothing compared to the nasty fall you saved me." Her voice was low, a little breathless.

He wanted to hear her speak again. "I bear responsibility, for startling you so. Do you have business with someone here?"

The door still stood wide open, the footman watching avidly from the threshold.

Her gaze passed over Will, and her forehead creased. "Are you..."

He bowed. "Will Archer, Esquire, at your service."

"You're a solicitor? I thought perhaps you were... I don't know.... one of the family."

Not if you ask either of the Carringtons.

She gestured at the knocker. "The house is in mourning?"

She had come to call without knowing of the Carringtons' loss? "Yes. Lord Carrington's son died. About six months ago."

"Oh." She sounded shocked. "How sad. But – six months, you said?"

"An only son," Will said dryly. "An only child, in fact. Lady Carrington is still – understandably – in full mourning."

"Of course. Still, I must..." She turned to the footman. "Is Lord Carrington at home?"

And you've been dismissed. Will shook his head a little, amused at himself for caring, and turned toward the street.

"I can inquire, Miss," Jenkins murmured. He was obviously waiting for a calling card, which seemed not to be forthcoming. Finally he said, "Who may I say is asking for him?"

"Miss Winslow," she said.

Will spun around so fast his head swam.

"Miss Althea Winslow," the girl went on. "Tell him, please, that I said he will certainly remember my mother. Anna Winslow."

* * *

The footman merely bowed and backed away. Thea had only an instant to wonder if he intended to close the door and leave her standing on the stoop, but Will Archer – who had acted so efficiently before to haul her up from a disastrous tumble down the stone steps – swept her into the house so quickly that she almost tripped over the footman's highly-polished shoes. She didn't have a chance to signal Alice, who was no doubt watching anxiously from across the street – probably convinced that the slavers had indeed snatched her from the very doorstep and she'd be off to a sultan's harem by morning.

After the sunlit outdoors, the entry hall was dim, and she had trouble focusing. All those windows, yet hardly a scrap of daylight had been allowed to enter the house. The Carringtons were in mourning, she reminded herself, wondering what had caused the death of their lost son.

"I'll tell his lordship about his visitor, Jenkins," Will Archer said briskly. "Miss Winslow, if you will just sit here for a moment..." He ushered her to a bench near the front door, then seemed to think better of it and, with a quick glance at the stairway, opened the door of a small reception room instead and almost thrust her inside. As he closed the door, she heard him say, "Make sure she doesn't vanish, Jenkins."

Thea frowned. He couldn't possibly know that she had hesitated on the stoop, debating what to do. She'd reached for the knocker twice, and twice she had let her hand drop before touching it. If the door hadn't opened just then, she might have backed away, lost her nerve, made an excuse to return another day. But for all he knew, she had just arrived and hadn't had time to knock. So why did he think she might walk away now?

Well, she wouldn't. She'd passed the first big hurdle. She was inside the house, and she was determined to achieve her goal. Now that she knew Lord Carrington was present, she would not leave without speaking to him. If he refused to see her, she would... she would...

She paced, too nervous to sit down. She'd tried to plan what she would say, but now that the moment was upon her, her mind had gone all aflutter.

Will Archer returned. For a moment he simply stood in the doorway, surveying her, curiosity gleaming in his eyes.

"Lord Carrington will see you in his bookroom."

Thea took a deep breath and followed him out of the reception room and across the dark entry to the back of the house, where a deeply-carved paneled door stood ajar. He tapped once, pushed the door wide, and stepped back to wave her in. "Miss Winslow to see you, sir."

A different sort of man might have called the room a library, because two walls were lined with bookshelves. So there was one thing she could deduce about Lord Carrington – he wasn't pretentious. Of course, the focus of the room was not the books, which looked too neatly lined up to be well-used, but the big desk. It sat at an angle to the fireplace so heat would channel directly to the man who worked there. It seemed he was also practical – and perhaps cold-blooded, as older people often were.

This room, too, was dim, lit mainly by the crackling coals in the grate and by a lamp which stood on the desk. Long windows at the back of the room were swathed in dark green velvet, with only a narrow strip of glass left bare to admit a weak patch of sunlight. The combination of light and dark threw odd shadows across the room and made it difficult for Thea to clearly see the man at the desk. His shoulders were wide, his face deeply lined and tired-looking. His hair was iron-gray, though it was as thick as that of a much younger man. Judging by the way he sat straight in his chair, he must be tall.

She swallowed annoyance when he didn't rise as a gentleman would have. He no doubt thought an earl owed no such courtesies to a mere miss. Or perhaps he suspected why she had come.

"Lord Carrington," she said, and made her curtsy just as Madame had taught her years ago.

He grunted. "This is not the court, and you are not making your bow before the king. Let us leave off the trimmings and have the meat, if you please." He looked past her to the young man. "I need nothing else from you, Archer. You may go."

Will Archer settled himself against the door and folded his arms across his chest. "It would be wise to have your solicitor present for this conversation, sir."

"I don't need a chaperone And if you're staying to gloat over your success, recollect that I asked you to find Anna Winslow, Archer. Not her daughter."

Thea blinked. Lord Carrington had looked for her mother? Actually tried to find her? Perhaps this conversation wasn't going to go at all the way she had anticipated.

"I believe, sir, that I have accomplished your purpose. Surely Miss Winslow can inform you of her mother's whereabouts. I assume you will then have further instructions for me, so I may as well stay and save you the effort of filling me in later."

"Nosy beggar, aren't you?" But Carrington didn't argue the point. "Well, Miss Winslow? What have you to say for yourself? Is Anna Winslow in truth your mother?"

"Yes, sir."

"And what of her other child? Her son?"

Thea frowned. "She had no other child. Only me." She shot a look over her shoulder at Will Archer and said carefully, "I was twenty-two years old last January."

Lord Carrington's hand clenched, the knuckles turning white. The pen he held cracked, and he dropped the pieces carelessly on the blotter. "A girl. Only a girl."

"My apologies, sir," she said tartly. "Perhaps you would care to know that my mother died four months ago." The words were still hard to say; voicing the fact seemed to make her loss even more painful.

Carrington waved a hand as if to swat away a fly – as though her mother's death mattered not at all to him.

And it probably didn't. Neither did Thea herself, for she was *only a girl.*

"You may go," he said.

From the corner of her eye, she saw Will Archer push away from the door. Did he intend to offer support, or to escort her out of the room? Not that it mattered. She didn't need to be defended, and she wouldn't be removed until she had said her piece. So much for discretion, though, and careful circumlocution intended to protect the feelings and the reputation of a man who, as it turned out, did not deserve such respect.

She took two steps closer, till she was leaning on the desk opposite Lord Carrington, staring down at him. His face was pasty-white in the glare of the desk lamp, a sharp contrast to the purplish bags under his eyes. He didn't meet her gaze.

"She never told me anything at all," Thea said. "I didn't know until after she died, when I found her papers, that she was a governess once. That she was employed in this very house to teach your son – until you seduced her and abandoned her. Turned her off without a reference, with nowhere to go. She kept your secrets, all her life. But I won't keep them, unless you make it worth my while – *Father*."

* * *

Will had seen it coming, of course. The instant Lord Carrington had asked – with that note in his voice which was almost hope – whether Anna had a son, he had known who this young woman must be.

But what the man was thinking was beyond his understanding. Did Carrington honestly believe he could simply set aside the rules of primogeniture just because he didn't want his title to go to a distant branch of the family, a branch he considered less than noble? Did he think he could set aside the centuries-long tradition of inheritances passed down to the firstborn legitimate male by somehow making it appear that a son born of a long-ago mistress was his true and legal heir?

Not that it mattered what he might have schemed to do, because – instead of a son – that long-ago mistress had given birth to this blackmailing hussy of a daughter. Will could hardly believe his first impression of her had been so wrong. *Make it worth my while,* indeed! What would Carrington say to *that*?

The earl growled. "You think to threaten me? Go ahead and tell the world, missy. What do I care what people think of me? But your reputation will be ruined indeed with this tale.

No man of family, of honor, of standing will have you."

She shrugged. "Do you think I don't know that? I have no wish to marry."

"Nonsense. Every female wants a husband. Marriage is the only thing they're fit for, and fripperies the only other things they can think of."

"Perhaps that is true of the women you know – ones who have no higher purpose. But I don't care about marriage."

Interesting that her voice had trembled a little. And what *higher purpose* was she talking about?

"You'd best care," Carrington said. "It's yourself you'll brand, not me, if you announce to the world that you're the by-blow of an earl. The illegitimate offspring of a peer's careless fling with a mere servant."

"She was not a servant." She braced her hands on the desk, bending closer, until her face was inches from Lord Carrington's and her breath actually stirred the old man's hair. "And obviously it was not a careless fling, or you wouldn't even have remembered her name, much less searched for her. Do not insult my mother by implying she was nothing special." Her voice was low, hard, unforgiving. "The fault is with you, not with her."

Carrington pulled back, and for an instant Will saw something odd in that hard face. Was it surprise? Even – perhaps – a touch of fear? He couldn't help admiring her spunk for standing up to the old man like that. In six months of working with Carrington, Will had never seen the earl flinch – till now, as he faced this young woman.

No question she's his daughter. That apple didn't fall far from the tree.

Will said quietly, "What is it you want, Miss Winslow?"

"That's a damn fool question. She wants money, of course." Carrington thrust his chair back from the desk and stood. "Not that I care what she wants. She gets nothing from me. See her out, Archer. No, *throw* her out." He strode over to a bookcase and pulled a volume off the shelf.

Will would have wagered his next month's income that it was no more than a prop, that the earl had no idea exactly which book he held.

Miss Winslow stood very still. Will held his breath, waiting for tears – but she seemed to have inherited the earl's pride as well as his determination. She drew her dignity closely around her like a second cloak. "Lord Carrington, you leave me with little choice."

Carrington grunted. "My intention was to leave you none at all." He stretched out a hand toward the bell pull. "Must I summon the footman to have you removed?"

Will moved a little closer to the young woman and lowered his voice. "He will do it, you know."

She turned her gaze on him. "What a popular solicitor you must be – if you're always so quick to agree with your master's wishes."

My master? From her perspective, it must indeed look as if he'd fallen meekly into line. *Don't argue with her.* "Do you wish to be carried out over Jenkins's shoulder? Surely you must see that it will do no good to persist just now."

"*Just now?* He does not seem the sort to ever repent a decision, once made."

It hadn't taken her long to sum up the old man. And why had Will said that, anyway? She was a self-confessed blackmailer. It was hardly his role as Carrington's solicitor to encourage her in any way. Still, perhaps a hint could move her out of the room, out of the house, away from this explosive situation.

"Perhaps if he has a little time to reflect," Will offered, "and to consider the fact that you alone now carry his blood..."

She snorted. "Are you truly that much of a fool, Mr. Archer?" She marched across the room to the door.

He hurried after her, catching up midway across the entry hall. "Miss Winslow, where can I find you?"

She swung round and stared up at him, her wide brown eyes brimming with disbelief. "Why would you want to?"

Because I can't afford to lose you.

He couldn't simply let her disappear. While she was right to think that Carrington seldom changed his mind once it was made up, Will suspected this situation might be different. The moment she was out of sight, the earl was apt to demand that Will produce her once more. "In case you're worried, I have no intention of setting the Runners on you for your attempt at blackmail."

"Let me assure you that I am more relieved than I can say." Her tone dripped disdain.

Jenkins had already opened the door for her, and she swept through it.

"Where can I reach you?" Will called after her. He followed her down to the pavement, where a neatly-dressed maid had fallen into step beside her. "If things should change."

"Oh, of course," she said over her shoulder. "I shall put all my confidence in you, Mr. Archer – because Lord Carrington obviously has such a high regard for you that of course he will yield to your persuasion!"

"I require your direction, Miss Winslow," he snapped. "Or do you want me to follow you?"

She didn't look back. "You're welcome to try," she called. "You might wish to retrieve your hat first, though, if you don't want people to stare."

"Damn," Will muttered and turned back for hat and walking stick.

Jenkins was holding them out, obviously doing his best not to grin.

A bellow echoed through the house. "Get that girl back here!"

Will pointed toward the corner of Grosvenor Square, where Miss Winslow and her maid were about to turn out of sight. "Go, Jenkins!"

The footman thrust Will's hat into his hands, but the stick went spinning across the stoop and into the bushes. He dashed down the stairs.

Will retrieved his walking stick, strolled back into the house, and laid his hat on the bench. Eyeing himself in the mirror over the mantel, he smoothed his hair where the breeze – or possibly his aggravation with Althea Winslow – had rumpled it. He was just finishing when Jenkins returned with the two young women.

Will turned to face Miss Winslow and smiled, enjoying the moment. "I believe I did say something about the wisdom of giving Lord Carrington an opportunity to reflect?"

She rolled her eyes.

He bowed. "After you, Miss Winslow. His lordship awaits."

* * *

There was no guessing what Lord Carrington had in mind, but Thea was pretty sure she knew what he wouldn't say. *Welcome to the family. What a joy it is to finally meet my daughter. What can I do to make things right, my dear?*

He had refused to listen, come agonizingly close to calling her mother a lightskirt, threatened bodily violence to throw her out, sent his footman to drag her back...

Though it had not been Lord Carrington but his tame lapdog of a solicitor who had actually dispatched the footman. Probably Will Archer was in such sad physical shape from sitting over a desk with his books all day that he knew he couldn't run fast enough to catch up with two young women who were accustomed to walking everywhere they went.

Of course, he didn't exactly look like a lump. He was a good eight inches taller than Thea, broad in the shoulders and trim everywhere else, without even a hint of a soft belly. In fact, the only thing that was soft about him seemed to be his dark hair, which had ruffled invitingly in the breeze.

She pulled herself back to the library. Had Lord Carrington said something? Was he waiting for an answer, or was he just staring silently at her, rudely looking her over from head to toe as though he was assessing a new horse for his stables? Yet another failure of manners, another infraction to resent.

"Hopeless," he said. "You look like a tradesman's brat."

"I could hardly dress the part of an earl's daughter on a teacher's wages," she snapped.

His eyes flared. "Don't get above yourself, missy. If you're going to have any connection with me, you'll behave yourself."

"I have not said I wish any connection with you, sir."

17

"I know – you only came for money. Well, you won't get it unless you follow my rules. Sit down, girl." His gaze shifted. "You, too, Archer. This concerns you as well."

The solicitor raised his eyebrows, but he didn't speak. He moved a chair toward the desk for Thea and waited for her to sit before settling himself.

Lord Carrington's gaze rested on Thea. "Twenty-two, you said."

"Last January, yes."

"And not yet married?"

"Certainly not."

"On the shelf, in fact."

"That is hardly—"

"Facts are facts, miss. If you'd been born on the right side of the blanket, you'd have been wed five years ago. Past time to take care of that. So since you've declared yourself my daughter—"

Althea was moved to protest. "It is not my declaration that makes it so, sir. Your own actions, decades ago, are what brought me here."

Lord Carrington waved a careless hand. "Hardly the point. I have just the bridegroom for you."

"*What*? No!"

Beside her, Will Archer stirred. "The lady has made clear that she has no desire to be wed."

Carrington didn't seem to hear either of them. "You'll marry my heir. Perfect solution. Get you off my hands, settle you for the future, and pass the title down through my bloodline after all."

Althea managed to get a breath. Was the man moonstruck? "I hardly think the heir to an earldom would be agreeable to marrying a female of questionable birth. You said yourself that no gentleman would ally himself with a female in my position."

"This one will. He's barely got a claim to being a gentleman himself. Right, Archer?" He didn't wait for an answer. "And considering I hold the purse strings, he'll fall into line. Oh, the estate is entailed, all right, but that only includes the manor house. Every bit of the rest – this house, the hunting box, the yacht, the other properties, the money invested in the funds – that fortune is mine alone, and it's up to me to decide who gets it after I stick my spoon in the wall."

Will Archer rubbed his temple as though it hurt.

"That's the ticket, then." Lord Carrington sounded pleased with himself. "Marry the heir, and I leave the lot to him. Then it'll be his responsibility to take care of you in style."

"Sir." The solicitor sounded hoarse. "Your simple promise is hardly adequate surety for such a large commitment."

"Wait a minute," Althea protested. "I never agreed – what do you mean, *such a large commitment*? Are you implying that marrying me would be such a horrible prospect that—"

"You could change your mind again tomorrow, sir."

"Are you questioning my word, boy?" Lord Carrington roared.

"Clarification in a written agreement would seem to be the least that anyone would require, sir."

She had to give Will Archer credit for not backing down. "This entire discussion is beside the point. Even were I interested in marriage—"

Lord Carrington glared. "You came here asking to be recognized as my daughter, so you'll do as you're told."

"I am not your property to coerce!"

"Sure about that, are you? All I have to do is claim you as my by-blow, and that gives me the power to marry you off to anyone I choose."

Thea had a sinking feeling he was absolutely right. She scrambled to regain lost ground. "Even assuming I was open to the notion of marriage at all, how could I possibly agree to marry someone I know nothing about?"

"Better him than your other options. As an illegitimate offspring, the best you could hope for would be some kind of a Cit, but I suppose if you'd rather have that than my heir—"

"I have not agreed to anything!" The old man really was quite astounding. Since pointing out that marriage was distasteful to her seemed to have had no impact on him, she'd try another direction. "What sort of a man is this heir of yours? What is his age, his nature? Does he even wish to marry? How close is the relationship? And how can you expect me to meekly accede to your wishes when this is a person I have never even met?"

"But you have."

"Agreed? I have *not—*"

"I mean you've met." The earl waved a careless hand and nodded toward Will Archer. "Daughter, let me present heir. Heir, daughter."

For just an instant, Thea wondered if Lord Carrington had a sense of humor after all. Turning toward the man sitting next to her, she tried to catch her breath. "You?"

Will Archer nodded. He seemed to have lost his voice.

"Special license, of course," his lordship went on, "and a wedding right away, so no one has a chance to ask questions. We'll say Miss Winslow is a distant cousin... or a ward, perhaps. Ward might be better, since Archer actually *is* a distant cousin. You might have a great-grandfather in common, perhaps – not nearly close enough to give you pause, missy."

"No," Will Archer said firmly. "The idea is out of the question."

Thea sat up straight. "Well, I never! I suppose you're too high in the instep to consider allying yourself with someone who can't claim her parents were married? What was all that about you being *barely a gentleman*, eh?"

He shot her a look that threatened to set her hair on fire. "Will you shush?"

He might have a point. Why bother to be annoyed at him for refusing the proposition when marrying him was the last thing she wanted to do? – No, it had nothing to do with him; her objection was to marrying at all. But if she let him take the blame and bear the heat of Lord Carrington's disapproval, she wouldn't have to.

"Sir," he went on. "I must insist on the ordinary provisions. It is only common sense to put everything in writing. To safeguard the rights of everyone, a marriage contract will need to specify all terms of the agreement. What about a dowry?"

"A marriage contract? A *dowry*?" Thea shrieked. "What happened to *The idea is out of the question*?"

Will Archer ignored her. "There would need to be provision for regular expenses, such as a suitable wardrobe for the lady. And for living arrangements as well. I hardly think you would want your ... uh... daughter living under the same roof as Lady Carrington, and my rooms at Lincoln's Inn are not at all suitable for a wife."

Thea stared at him, stunned.

"Oh, we can work all that out," Lord Carrington said. "It's all just details anyway, now that the agreement's made."

Thea gasped. "But I never agreed—"

"Yes, yes. That's why these things are best left to the men, Miss..." Lord Carrington paused. "What did you say your Christian name is?"

The library door opened and a tall, gaunt woman in black stalked in. "Who, sir, is the maid sitting in the entryway, and why is she muttering about slavers and harems? In fact, why is she in the house at all?" She paused as her gaze fell on Will Archer. "Oh. It's you again."

"Ma'am," Carrington said, "you must treat the heir with respect."

Thea's jaw dropped at the sheer hypocrisy of the man.

Will Archer caught her eye and shrugged.

"He's come to present his betrothed to me," the earl went on. "Not a well-thought-out action, of course. Would have been smarter to come by himself first and get my approval of the match, but no, he just brought her along. You know, it could have been quite embarrassing, my boy, springing her on me like that."

He sounded so jocular Thea thought she might just be sick.

"But fortunately she seems to fit the bill. Lady Carrington, Miss Winslow. I'm sure you two will have a wonderful time getting to know each other."

Lady Carrington's glare swept over Thea. "Doubtful. You are surely not planning to invite them to dinner, my lord."

"Of course not, my dear. They have far too much to do, getting ready for a wedding. Run along now, children." Lord Carrington sounded almost jovial. "I'll see you tomorrow, Archer, and we'll take up the matter of the marriage contracts."

Chapter Two

Will wouldn't have expected anything to keep Althea Winslow from expressing her opinion, but as she walked along Grosvenor Square, she said nothing at all. Or, more accurately, she didn't verbalize, because the direction of her thoughts was quite clear from the way her heels struck against the cobblestones in a fast, hard rhythm which must have sent shudders up to her knees at least.

He cleared his throat and ventured, "I actually wasn't agreeing with him."

She glared up at him and cast a quick look over her shoulder at the maid. "It is quite unnecessary for you to accompany us, Mr. Archer. It is a long walk and Alice and I do not require protection."

"I could not call myself anything like a gentleman if I allowed you to wander across the city on your own."

"Apparently, you cannot call yourself anything like a gentleman under any circumstances."

Now that was hardly fair. "Lord Carrington has an interesting view of the aristocracy's rules. You must realize I've dealt with him for much longer than you have, Miss Winslow. When it comes to his lordship, it never pays to assume anything. And you and I do have rather a lot to discuss."

"Not now. Not here."

"Fine." He raised a hand to summon a hansom.

"I have no funds to pay for rides."

"Fortunately, I can manage the expense." He handed her into the cab, offered assistance to the maid to follow, and – disregarding Miss Winslow's fiery look – pointed out calmly, "The driver needs to know your destination, and I cannot enlighten him because you have still not told me where to find you."

She would have argued, he thought, but the maid perked up. "It's Madame Beauchamp's School on Charlotte Street, right off Bedford Square."

Surely Miss Winslow was too old to still be in school? But no, she'd said something about a teacher's wages. Perhaps she had taken after her mother, as well as her father. Surely his first impression couldn't have been entirely wrong and she had a softer side... hidden somewhere.

She didn't look the part of a termagant. She was pretty enough, with an oval face, creamy skin, rich chestnut-brown hair that flashed with red highlights where her bonnet let the sun touch it. No doubt her looks had come from her mother, because the only part of her that resembled his lordship was that firm chin. And the way her mouth set into a line when she had made up her mind.

Will instructed the coachman. As the man clucked to his horse, Will swung into the carriage and smiled broadly at the maid. "Thank you for the information, Alice."

The maid beamed. "My word, sir, this is a treat! We walked all the way here, you know, and..."

"Alice, Mr. Archer does not wish to hear about our walk."

He ignored Miss Winslow and focused on the maid. "All the way from Bedford Square? What a long walk, indeed. Do tell me about the school, Alice."

"Oh, it's ever so nice, sir. Madame came here from France after the Terror, you know, and started the school. Most of the young ladies are day students, but a few board with us all the time. They study all sorts of things – some interesting ones and some not-so-interesting, if you take my meaning."

He was far more intrigued by the teachers than by the students or the curriculum. "And Miss Winslow is one of the instructors?"

"Oh, yes, sir, she teaches etiquette and deportment and manners and–"

He tried to swallow his smile at the idea of Althea Winslow – the same fishwife who without an instant's hesitation had confronted the Earl of Carrington – teaching young ladies the proper way to behave. "Indeed? I would give a pretty penny to sit in on those lessons."

Alice laughed. "Oh, no, sir, gentlemen aren't allowed inside Madame's school."

"Of course not. The young ladies' parents would be horrified."

Miss Winslow stirred and muttered, "And where, pray tell, would you get that pretty penny? From your negotiations with his lordship?"

"Don't underestimate me, Miss Winslow."

"Oh, I can see you have hidden depths of guile."

"You're quite difficult to please, you know. First you accuse me of being too agreeable to my clients' whims, and now you seem unhappy that I stood up to his lordship and insisted on negotiating a—"

"That's enough, Mr. Archer." She sat up straight. "We'll get out here, Alice, and walk the rest of the way. It will take us only a few minutes now."

"As you wish," Will said agreeably. "A stretch of the legs sounds quite inviting, and Alice's description of the school is so intriguing I simply must see it. At least the exterior, even if I cannot be admitted." He rapped the top of the carriage, and the driver pulled off to the edge of the street.

By the time he'd paid the fare, the maid was almost out of sight, but Miss Winslow waited primly on the walk. "I sent Alice ahead to the greengrocer to see if there is any fruit available at end-of-day prices, since it appears your intention is to stick to me like a burr."

"Until we complete our very necessary conversation, yes." Will offered his arm.

She laid her fingertips on his sleeve. "And since I do not plan to have that conversation within the hearing of anyone associated with Madame's school—"

"What a very good idea. I must say I appreciate you choosing the open air, where yelling would be so very noticeable, to conduct this discussion."

"I do not yell."

"Of course not," Will said mildly. "You merely express your opinions. Strongly. It is an approach that I think you had best learn does not accomplish much with Lord Carrington."

He thought she wasn't going to answer, but finally she said, "How long have you known him?"

"Only since the death of his son. Before that, my branch of the family had essentially nothing to do with the earldom, or with the earl. We truly are only distant cousins, as he said. I have never been invited to visit the manor, in Hampshire. In fact, though I have clients all around Grosvenor Square, I had not been inside the earl's house until after I became his heir."

"But now you do his legal work?"

"Just the search for your mother – and it is clear, now, why he started that search only after Robert's death, and why he didn't turn the job over to his regular solicitors. And why he didn't confide the entire truth to me, for that matter. I had no idea until today why he was looking for her."

"Because he knew she was with child when he turned her out."

"I can draw no other conclusion."

She walked along in silence for a bit. "And if I had been a male, he would have tried to displace you."

"It seems so."

"What was his name?" Her voice wavered just a little. "My... my brother."

"Robert. He bore the courtesy title of Lord Calvert, from the viscountcy that Lord Carrington holds."

"Yes, I do know how the rules of aristocratic titles function." She bit her lip. "I'm sorry, I shouldn't snap at you. It's hardly your fault that only a few months ago I discovered that I even had a brother... a half-brother, I mean. And now I find that I shall never have a chance to know him."

"From all the reports, I doubt you would have enjoyed his acquaintance."

"Like his father, was he?"

"It seems so, though I've never heard it said that Lord Carrington was a gamester."

"And Robert was?"

"I could not say for certain, not having moved in those exalted circles."

"But now you will, as the heir."

"Inheriting is not something I asked for, or dreamed of. Finding myself under Lord Carrington's thumb is not a pleasant prospect."

"But now you wish me to be there as well. Under his thumb – answering to him."

"Not at all. I see this as an opportunity for both of us."

"*Marriage*?"

"Look, Miss Winslow. You came to see your father today for a reason. Why not four months ago, when you first found out about him?"

She tipped her chin a little higher. "My mother's death—"

"But why today? His lordship was right about one thing. You want money, or you wouldn't have come within miles of the man who betrayed and abandoned your mother."

"Apparently I'm not the only one who is thinking about money. You seemed quite anxious to get your hands on my hypothetical dowry."

Will shrugged. "It's true I would benefit from access to funds, though in my case, it's not for me personally but for the estate. If I am to be saddled with Monkscroft—"

"That's the name of the estate?"

"You didn't look it up before seeking him out? It was an abbey, before the Dissolution, when it came to the Archer family from King Edward."

"If you've finished with the history lesson, Mr. Archer..."

"Very well. I'm sure, now that you've met him, you realize that in his pique in losing the direct line of succession, Lord Carrington is capable of leaving all his unentailed property to found a home for—" He paused, at a loss.

"Elderly cats," she suggested.

"Or something just as outrageous. If I have no choice but to step into his shoes, to become the next Earl of Carrington, I would just as lief have the necessary means to carry out the role."

"To be a gentleman of fashion, you mean?"

27

"To be a good landlord, a good steward of the family's heritage." He felt a little pompous, saying it out loud for the first time – but it was true.

"The estate must support itself and more, or where did he get the money to buy hunting boxes and yachts and houses in Grosvenor Square, and to invest in the funds?"

"Properties like Monkscroft may have enriched their owners in the past, but if the experience of my other clients is anything to go by, things are different these days."

"But you don't know for certain… because he hasn't shared that information? And I'm sure you don't dare ask." Her tone was thoughtful. "What a shame – because if you *did* ask, perhaps he'd get annoyed with you for pressing too hard and he'd leave it all to me instead."

Will choked down a laugh. "You can try to charm him into it, but I wouldn't care to wager on your success."

"You don't think I can be charming?"

"It's not that," he said, as tactfully as he could manage. "I don't think he's susceptible to charm – and I know damned well he doesn't believe women are suited to handle money."

"I don't see how all that makes a marriage contract a good idea."

"Not the contract. The *negotiation* of a marriage contract. That kind of detailed discussion can take months, and given enough time, his mind will no doubt have turned to other things. In the meanwhile, surely I can convince him that his daughter, my prospective bride, cannot walk around London dressed like a tradesman's brat, and get you a clothing allowance, at least. Will that be enough to take care of your needs?"

"I don't know. Is a thousand guineas a reasonable clothing allowance?"

Will nearly staggered. "A *thousand* – what in the devil do you need that kind of money for? Gambling debts?"

"Madame's school," she said. "The owner wants to sell the building, and he has an offer from a prospective buyer. If we can't match the bid, the school will have to move."

"And there's no money to do that either?"

"It was not something Madame planned for, especially not now that my mother is gone." Her throat worked as though saying the words had hurt. "My mother was not only a teacher but a partner in the endeavor. I am trying to step into her place, but she taught a great number of subjects and I am not yet qualified to deal with advanced students. We've already hired two teachers to replace her, and we need at least one more."

"That must be putting a strain on the budget."

She nodded. "The only alternative, if we cannot buy the building and we cannot afford to move, is to close the school. But that would leave Madame with nothing to show for all her years of hard work – and with nothing to live on."

"And it would leave you with nothing from your mother's partnership as well."

"I don't care about an inheritance, but I would be without employment. Finding another position would not be easy. And I'd also be without a home, since the school is the only one I remember." The words were calm, but her voice trembled just a little. "And here we are, at Madame's school." Her hand dropped from his sleeve. "Thank you for your escort, sir, and for the explanation of your thinking and your motives. I still believe you are misguided, but—"

Will looked past her to a four-story building with a discreet sign above the door, marking it as Madame Beauchamp's School for Young Ladies. The original red bricks of the facade showed through here and there, where the cream-colored paint of a later era had worn thin. But the door bore a fresh coat of deep blue, and the steps had been scrubbed till they almost shone. The building was across Charlotte Street and down just a bit from the corner of Bedford Square, which formed an inviting green oasis for the surrounding townhouses.

"May I call on you tomorrow," he asked, "after my discussion with his lordship? Or is Alice correct that no gentleman can be admitted under any circumstances?"

Four very young ladies came down the street, two by two and arm in arm. They paused, eyeing Will and Thea. "You have a gentleman caller, Miss Winslow?" one of them said. "Coo!"

Her walking partner elbowed her. "*Coo* is not proper language, Tish."

"Ladies," Will said, sweeping off his hat and bowing.

The girls giggled and showed every indication of wanting to stay right there to watch, until Miss Winslow gave them a long, direct look. Even then, they dawdled up the steps, looking back over their shoulders.

So the idea of Miss Winslow receiving gentlemen callers was unusual enough to be worthy of note. Not that it mattered to Will, of course, though it might have if he had considered for even one moment actually marrying the girl.

Which of course he hadn't. And wouldn't. This whole negotiation was going nowhere; he would make certain of it.

"Tomorrow," she said finally, and without a look back, she followed the girls to the front door.

Will watched her out of sight, and then, with a sigh, went to look for a hansom to take him on to Lincoln's Inn. He had a great deal of reading and thinking and planning to do before his meeting with Lord Carrington on the morrow.

* * *

But it was not to the Carrington town house that Will went, late the next morning, but to another of the great establishments along Grosvenor Square. The butler showed him to a small sitting room favored by the lady of the house, and he took a chair near the fire. As he awaited his client's pleasure, he dug out from his briefcase the list he had made last night, working until his desk lamp had burned the last of its oil supply and his eyes had grown grainy with tiredness.

He was so focused on the upcoming negotiation with Carrington that he didn't hear his client's approach until the old lady spoke from the doorway. "Well, Mr. Archer – and don't you look a fright this morning."

Her voice grated on his ears, reminding him of carriage wheels crunching across gravel. He jumped to his feet, his briefcase and the list flying off his knee. "Good morning, Lady Stone. My apologies."

"For what? I'm the one who's late for our appointment. The builder I've hired to repoint the chimneys insisted on talking to me rather than to my butler, and he – the builder, I mean, not the butler – is very long-winded." She swept into the room and settled in a chair across from his. The pointed toes of her shoes, peeking out under the lace trim of a walking dress which would have been more suitable for a woman half her age, nearly touched the paper he'd dropped. Her beady black gaze devoured the careful script. "You're working on a marriage contract? For whom, dear boy?"

"My clients' business is confidential, my lady."

"Oh, now where's the fun in making me ask around? And do you really want to ruin my reputation for knowing all the *on dits* before anyone else does? There's a reason I'm known as the most unrepentant gossip in the *ton*, you know."

He knew. There was a rumor that Lady Stone's nose had not been nearly so long or so pointed before she began sticking it into everyone else's business. Will had his doubts about that, though. Not because she wasn't a gossip – for she absolutely was – but because he was fairly sure there had never been a time when she *hadn't* poked into things that were none of her affair – so perhaps she had actually been born with that beak of a nose, and the bump of curiosity that seemed to come with it.

"Do tell me what it is you'd like me to do for you, Lady Stone."

Her lips formed a little pout. Good lord, was the woman actually trying to *flirt*? "Well, it was worth an attempt," she murmured. "But if you're going to be difficult about it, very well. I want you to review the agreement about the chimneys."

"If you don't trust the builder, why did you hire him?"

"I never trust anyone who gets above himself. How dare he demand to speak to me personally? Does he not believe I will pay my bills?"

It must be only a rhetorical question, for Lady Stone must know even better than Will did how many of the aristocratic families seemed to never catch up on their financial obligations.

She had gone straight on. "And I believe I will need to make an arrangement for my companion."

"I thought we finished that bit of business."

"We did, for the last girl. This one is new, and it appears she has already found a young man to catch her eye. It seems I cannot keep a companion, no matter what I do."

"If you didn't matchmake and then provide an income for each one, perhaps one would stay with you."

"But it amuses me so to make certain that my girls always have pin money, independent from their husbands. And even better, it drives my nephew to distraction as he watches me disperse my personal funds to the winds, as he calls it. He thinks I should leave it all to him."

Will felt a tinge of heat rise in his face. Did he himself sound just a bit like the current Lord Stone, whining about a relative's perceived unfairness over money? But the situations were not the same. Lady Stone's late husband had left his nephew and heir well-provided for, with not only a healthy estate in the country but a considerable fortune in the Funds. The money her ladyship was supposedly frittering away was her own, inherited from her mother's family.

Besides, her amusements, as she called them, cost her less than most ladies of fashion spent on their wardrobes each year. If it made her happy and it didn't cut into her capital, why shouldn't she do as she pleased? If she enjoyed making life easier for a series of young women who had for even a short while taken care of all the tasks Lady Stone despised doing for herself...

"—and of course that is why I would dearly love to read that marriage contract you're working on, to be certain I'm giving my young friends the best possible advice." She bent to reach for the page at her feet.

Will set his boot on the paper. "I'm sorry. What?"

She leaned back in her chair, her gaze steady. "Mr. Archer, I don't know where you've traveled to just now, but if you wouldn't mind coming back to our meeting..."

"So sorry, my lady. I... well, actually, I was thinking of a... but that's of no consequence. What sort of a settlement do you have in mind this time?"

"Oh, that's not really important. Just use the last one as an example, and let's move on to more interesting topics." Her eyes gleamed. "Thinking about your young lady, were you?"

"Why would you assume that?"

"Because when your mind wandered, it could hardly have been to anything other than a female, since we were speaking of companions and settlements and marriage contracts. Furthermore, because it's not at all like you to get lost in thought in the midst of a conference with a client, it must be a personal, intimate connection. Do tell me about her."

That was the last thing he could do. Confide in the most notorious gossip in London?

The beady gaze focused even more tightly on him, and the beak seemed to grow sharper. "Mr. Archer." The grating voice grew softer, gentler, almost hypnotic. "I treasure my reputation as a gossip, that is true. But I am very careful when I like the people who are involved. And I do like you, Mr. Archer. So tell me." She settled back in her chair, clearly intending to stay. "Would I like your young lady as well? And just what sort of trouble is she in?"

* * *

Will Archer hadn't mentioned a time for his call, but as the day dragged on, Thea found herself growing more tense, more annoyed, and more irritable. Did he think she was so trusting that she would put her faith in him to handle this entire debacle? Her life was at stake!

Of course, his was as well. Not that she cared about *that*, of course.

She was so preoccupied she almost forgot to join Madame at afternoon tea. The role – part honor, part responsibility – had been her mother's until Anna's death. Even four months later, Thea was still overwhelmed by the idea of being Madame's right hand, taking her mother's place as the two of them conferred about the young ladies under their care. Who was doing well in her studies, and who was falling behind. Who was a discipline problem, and who was inclined to be silly and focused on boys rather than books. Whether they could raise tuition costs by even a little, and if they could go on educating the charity students whose parents could afford to pay nothing.

And the ultimate question, the one Thea was afraid even to think about, much less enunciate: Whether the school could continue to operate at all, or if it would have to close.

If only her mother was still there. Anna had been as unflappable as Madame, always steady, solid, dependable. By comparison, Thea felt like a pillar of salt in a rainstorm. Every decision, every question seemed to splash against her, washing away a bit of her substance.

Thea would have missed her mother no matter what; Anna had been her rock, her best friend, and her framework for dealing with the world. But Madame's reliance on her made the hole left by Anna's passing even larger and more terrifying.

"Mr. Ballard called by again this morning." Madame refilled Thea's tea cup. "His potential buyer seems to be growing impatient for his decision."

"What did you tell him?"

"As you suggested, I hinted we just need another month or two. But I don't think he believed me, and it would be no wonder when I don't believe it myself. If we're not able to give him an answer right now, why would we be in any better circumstances in a few months?"

Thea's heart was pounding. "And what did he say?"

"He agreed to hold off the buyer for two more weeks, but he can give us no longer than that. And he hinted that we will need to make the delay worth his while. Althea, I know you went to see Lord Carrington yesterday. If you'd been successful, you would have come to me immediately with the good news."

"He was...difficult."

"I did warn you he was likely to be," Madame said gently.

"But I haven't given up yet. There are still possibilities."

"Which I don't suppose you'd like to tell me about."

"Not exactly," Thea admitted.

Alice tapped at the door of Madame's sitting room and put her head in. "Miss Thea, you have a caller." Her eyes were dancing; some mischief was clearly afoot.

Thea jumped to her feet, relief surging through her – followed immediately by trepidation. What would Will have to report? Perhaps not much at all; he had said this sort of discussion could drag out for months. Still, if he had been able to win a concession or two, perhaps he had even wangled enough money from Lord Carrington to solve the problem of the school. She knew she shouldn't get her hopes up, but... "If you'll excuse me, Madame. I had better see this caller quickly."

"Before the girls get wind of him," Alice said under her breath.

Madame raised an eyebrow. "A gentleman, Althea?"

Will Archer is more of a gentleman than Lord Carrington is, regardless of what his lordship thinks.

"You seem quite eager to greet him, my dear. You're smiling, and you appear to be a little breathless."

That *was* an odd reaction – but trust Madame to notice. It seemed that the mere fact Will had come had improved Thea's mood immeasurably. Still, she had no time to think about that just now. "Lord Carrington's solicitor said he would call today, Madame. He may have news for us."

"I see. Then by all means..." Madame waved Thea away.

Thea found Will on the stoop, leaning against a pillar that accented the small pediment over the door, arms folded across his chest. "I see Alice wasn't exaggerating when she said no males were allowed admittance to Madame's school," he said calmly.

"Rarely. Fathers or guardians, when they're making arrangements for their daughters' education, or paying their tuition, or coming to collect them, are allowed, but gentlemen callers are not encouraged. Madame feels it wise to set a good example for the girls. Shall we walk, Mr. Archer?"

He pushed himself away from the pillar. "Regardless of the

rules, it is reassuring to find you in such a hurry to greet me that you came out before your bonnet is properly tied."

Thea's hand went to the loose ribbon fluttering under her chin, and she took a moment to fix the bow. "My rush is only to get you off the property before the more susceptible of our young ladies attempt to practice their wiles on you."

"Of course," he murmured. "I must not get above myself by thinking you might have been impatient to see me." They walked a full minute in silence before he spoke again. "It is a comfort, though, to know you wish to protect me from the dangers of... ahem... young ladies."

Aggravating man. And she'd given him credit for being a gentleman! "Do you have news for me, Mr. Archer?"

"I did say this would likely be a prolonged negotiation."

Her heart sank. "Nothing? But I don't have unlimited time. Madame has just told me the building will be sold in two weeks."

She glanced over her shoulder at the school, still just visible though they had walked well down the street. Will was looking past the buildings lining Charlotte Street, his gaze seeming to rest on Montagu House, home of the British Museum. "Surely the new owner would not put you out the moment the sale was made. He might even appreciate having a tenant already established."

"If that was the case, I think we'd have been told. And I expect even if we can stay, the new owner would have to increase the rental payments substantially in order to make his investment pay for itself. We can't afford a higher rent any more than we can the purchase price."

"It does seem rather a steep price to pay for an ordinary building. Is there something very special about the premises?"

Thea shook her head. "If there is, it's something neither Madame nor I are aware of. But it seems unlikely. The school has been here for the last twenty years."

"Perhaps there is something that has escaped your notice because you are so familiar with the place, but that the buyer saw as special."

"That would be difficult to believe, since the buyer has not made a personal inspection."

"And you would know if he had, because of the rule about no males wandering around the premises." Will frowned. "Are you quite certain this buyer exists? Perhaps the current owner simply wants to sell and is taking this way to frighten you into purchasing the property at a higher price than he could otherwise hope for."

"I doubt Mr. Ballard has the imagination to come up with such a scheme."

"Then perhaps it is the location itself which makes the property a tempting bargain. The price is a thousand, you said?"

"No, but Mr. Ballard has indicated we would have to offer significantly more than the current bid to win out. And then there are certain crucial repairs we would have to make."

"I'd think the current owner should do that."

"Madame has discussed it with him, but he has been reluctant, under the circumstances. He seems to think she's finding flaws in an attempt to drive the price down. If only he could see the buckets in the attic, catching drips."

"She won't make an exception to her rule for him to see the damage?"

"Of course she would, but he has declined to come and look for himself."

"I suppose as long as he hasn't seen the leaks, he can pretend they don't exist – and he can sell the building without additional investment. I wonder what the buyer would think, if these *crucial repairs* were called to his attention."

"Unfortunately, I have no idea who the buyer is. And all this speculation is not productive." Thea took a deep breath. "Did you make any progress at all with his lordship?"

"He agreed to pay for new clothing that is more suitable to your station."

"Well, that's something." She brightened. "Perhaps if it's a significant sum, Mr. Ballard would accept it as a payment in earnest and at least delay his agreement with the other buyer."

"I think you misunderstand. Lord Carrington did not provide money. He instructed me to bring him the bills, and he will then advance the funds."

"You really are not much use at all as a solicitor, are you? What good is that to me? I don't need dresses."

"You do, actually. At least one gown, for I have accepted a dinner engagement for us."

"I am not going to sit down to dinner at Lord Carrington's table. And even if I were to agree to attend such an event, the clothing I already own would be perfectly good enough. Nothing I could possibly wear would win Lady Carrington's approval, and that man... my father... cannot pretend to be surprised by my wardrobe."

"The invitation did not come from the Carringtons. It will be a small dinner party, given by one of my clients."

Thea stopped walking. "Why am I invited?"

"The lady has indicated an interest in meeting you. It will probably be just Lady Stone and her current companion, so your lack of a chaperone will not be an issue."

"Lady Stone, hmm? Is she well-off? I wonder if she would like to be the patroness of a school."

"I doubt it. She is hardly a model for the education of the young."

"I don't need a model, I need *funds*," Thea muttered. "Why is she interested in me?"

"Her motivations are a mystery to me – as well as to most of the people around her, I believe. But you should feel flattered. She is choosy about her guests – she says she invites only those she finds to be amusing. This is the first time I have been invited to dine with her, and it is because of you."

"You're not amusing enough on your own to suit her? What did you tell this woman about me?"

He didn't stammer, or hesitate, or turn red, so Thea didn't know quite why she was so certain that her question made him uneasy. "I told her that you stood in need of a friend."

"That is not reassuring."

"I believe she may be able to help pressure Lord Carrington to–"

"*You told her?*"

"Of course not. I said nothing about your origins. But of

course she knows Lord Carrington, and she is quite powerful in the *ton*."

"She doesn't sound the sort to go around making friends with poor teachers. Why on earth would she be interested in me?"

Will cleared his throat. "Because, during my conference with her, she pressed me about why I was somewhat preoccupied."

Thea considered that. She felt just a bit charmed by his awkward admission that she had been the cause of his distraction. "You were trying to counsel a client but you were thinking about me instead?"

"I was thinking about the negotiations."

"Of course," she said flatly. *Foolish girl, to think it might have been you that stole his thoughts!*

"Miss Winslow, right now Lord Carrington holds all the power. At least, he believes he does, which has very much the same effect on the situation. He sees no need to make concessions, so he is at present reluctant to enter into serious negotiations. Again today, he simply stated his demands – an immediate marriage by special license, and acceptance of his word that at his death all of his unentailed property will come to us."

"Don't you mean, it will come to you?"

"Technically, yes, but..."

"Never mind. And if we don't agree to his demands?"

"Then – as he threatened yesterday – he will announce his sudden discovery of a daughter and have his regular solicitors open negotiations for your marriage to anyone who is interested in an alliance with an earl, even if that alliance comes via an unorthodox route."

"It's an empty threat." Thea shivered, nevertheless. "He wouldn't do that, because he can't want Lady Carrington to know the truth about me."

"Do you believe she is unaware? Would she not remember the names of all her son's governesses – especially one who was suddenly let go for no doubt mysterious reasons?"

"I hadn't thought of that."

"Perhaps it doesn't matter whether she knows or not.

Nevertheless, we need something to strengthen our position with the earl."

"I wonder..."

"I'm open to ideas," Will prompted.

"No, I was just thinking that maybe he wasn't always so awful. Living with her would make anyone sour."

"Quite possible – not that the observation is of much help. About the dinner party..."

Thea sighed. "I don't suppose it can hurt to go."

"Your enthusiasm is so encouraging," Will said dryly. "I can rearrange my morning to escort you to the modiste."

And what fun that would be. She wondered if he even knew anything useful about women's fashions... and if he did, where he might have learned it. "Do you have sisters?"

"No. Why?"

"I just wondered." Perhaps he had a mistress... Could a London solicitor afford a mistress?

Why had her mind wandered to that question?

"Tomorrow morning?" Will prompted.

Ah, yes, the modiste. "Even if I didn't have obligations of my own, I couldn't bear to take you away from your far-more-important engagements. In any case, I think I can manage something suitable to wear – since it is to be, as you said, a small and informal gathering."

He looked doubtful.

"Have no worries, Mr. Archer. I'll be certain to hand you the bill to pass along to Lord Carrington." And since the likelihood was that neither the solicitor not the earl had any idea what a dinner gown actually cost, she could ask Madame's regular seamstress to double the price on the invoice so she could put the extra toward the needs of the school. Every shilling would help.

Perhaps she could make this work after all.

Chapter Three

Thea expected Will to call to take her to Lady Stone's dinner in yet another hansom cab – she'd spent more time riding in cabs in the last few days than in the previous several years. So she was startled when a gleaming black barouche pulled up in front of the school, drawn by a pair of matched chestnut horses and driven by a uniformed coachman.

Despite her best efforts at discretion, word had spread through the school that Miss Winslow was going to a party, so at least half of the student boarders were lined up by the windows, jockeying for the best view and commenting on the quality of the horses, the elegance of the livery, and the looks of the young man who leaped down from the carriage and strolled up to the door.

"There's a coat of arms on the carriage," one of them exclaimed. "Miss Winslow, is your gentleman a lord?"

Not my gentleman. And he's only a future lord – though he does rather look the part tonight.

"I believe that must be my hostess's barouche," she said. "She seems quite intent on proper behavior. Notice, ladies, that the top is laid back so the carriage is open to the air – which makes it acceptable for me, as an unmarried lady, to ride through the city with a gentleman without a chaperone accompanying us."

The girls seemed to dismiss the etiquette lesson in favor of admiring the cut of Will's bottle-green coat – but at least they had enough command of themselves not to comment aloud on the fit of his pantaloons. And at least they weren't discussing how Thea's advanced age – in their eyes – put her beyond any consideration of needing a chaperone.

She gave up the attempt at teaching and gathered up her reticule and cloak while Alice went to answer the door.

"You're getting quite a sendoff," Will said as he settled her comfortably in the barouche. "The young ladies lining the windows, I mean. Shall I tip my hat to them?"

"Oh, please do not encourage their behavior. They're already quite man-mad enough." She eyed him. "And don't take that as a hidden compliment to your charms, sir – they're so undiscriminating as to practice flirting with the fishmonger's boy, if they happen to encounter him while they're out for a walk."

"I am duly chastened." He didn't sound it, however.

"You seem quite at home with the carriage and the servants," she commented finally.

"Hardly. As a solicitor living in chambers, I have no need of a carriage and team, nor anywhere to stable them even if I could afford such a luxury."

"It was very kind of Lady Stone to offer," Thea said tonelessly. What a stickler the woman must be, though, to insist on sending her own open carriage in order to preserve the proprieties. Suddenly she was looking forward to the evening with even less enthusiasm.

"Do you ride?" Will asked. "I don't keep a horse of my own, either, but there are livery stables nearby when I feel the urge."

"I've never learned." She had also never felt the lack, even though on occasion she had listened as her mother reminisced fondly of her own youthful days, when she and her brothers and sisters had shared a patient old nag. Growing up in London, in financial circumstances that required careful consideration of every expenditure, hadn't offered such opportunities to Thea. "But then I can't imagine needing to."

Sooner than she expected, the carriage clattered to a halt. A footman ran from the house and opened the low door. Will helped her down, and Thea looked around in surprise. "You didn't tell me we were coming back to Grosvenor Square. I do hope the Carringtons won't be coming and going this evening, or looking out the windows."

"With those heavy drapes? As for their movements – he goes to his clubs, I believe, but as far as I know, Lady Carrington doesn't go out at all."

"How long does she intend to carry on with her mourning?"

"I've never had what could be called a conversation with her at all, much less one that would give me a hint into the inner workings of her mind. Anyway, you're the expert on deportment. Isn't six months the custom, when one loses a child?"

Lady Stone's house was ablaze with candlelight, and her companion awaited them in a long drawing room where a fire burned cheerfully at each end, taking the chill out of the evening. Thea was glad to see that the young woman's dress was very similar to her own newly-altered one – a solid color that wasn't so bright it called attention to itself, made in a fairly plain fashion that was not excessively low in the neckline. Her own gown was a dark enough blue, so close to being gray, that it shouldn't raise too many eyebrows – since she was still technically in mourning for her mother. But the puffed sleeves and the hem finished with a ruffle of the same fabric made it feel suitable for a party.

"I'm Miss Harper," the companion offered. "Lady Stone asked me to make you comfortable because she has been slightly delayed. Sherry? Or something stronger, Mr. Archer?"

They accepted sherry and made small talk, and within a few minutes a tall, thin, almost gaunt woman swept into the room and settled in a wingback chair by one of the fires. "Now you must come and entertain me, Miss Winslow," she said. "Mr. Archer and Miss Harper are already acquainted, so we can leave them to themselves for a bit." She surveyed Thea, her beady eyes glistening. "And you're the young woman who has captured Mr. Archer's attention. I do hope you're going to tell me how you accomplished that."

Thea hadn't known quite what to expect, but it surely was not this woman – quite old, but with the intent, interested gaze of a much younger female.

"Mr. Archer tells me you're a teacher," Lady Stone went on. "What is it you teach, and where?"

"A little of everything now, to our younger students at Madame Beauchamp's School – though until lately I have instructed mostly in deportment, manners, and etiquette. Our students are mostly the daughters of tradesmen, so the quality of their training at home has been uncertain. Even lacking, sometimes."

"That must be quite an interesting challenge, since I presume some do not wish to learn."

"True enough, my lady, though it is usually effective to remind them that gentlemen are not impressed by young women without manners."

The old woman gave a bray of a laugh. "That is an all-purpose whip to keep them in line, I'm sure. The school seems very close to your heart. It is in Bedford Square?"

It seemed Will hadn't been quite accurate when he said he had told Lady Stone almost nothing about her. "Just off the square. And yes, it's very important to me. I grew up in the school, because my mother was a teacher there all my life." Was it possible that after all this woman might be the salvation, the angel, they needed? Will might have been wrong about that, too.

Before she could find words to ask, Lady Stone swept on. "Your mother, yes – Mr. Archer tells me that she has recently passed on. I'm so sorry for your loss. But surely you're not entirely alone in the world. Who are your people?"

"My mother came from Derbyshire," Thea said steadily. "Her father was a vicar, the younger son of a baronet there – not a noble family, but that of a gentleman."

"Winslow..." Lady Stone mused. "I think I knew some Winslows, and I seem to remember they were from that part of the country. But no, how foolish of me. That couldn't have been your maternal grandfather's surname, since it's yours."

Heat rose in Thea's face. Oh, why hadn't she realized the questions that would be asked, and the mess that attending a simple dinner in the *ton* would lead to?

"And your father's people?"

She swallowed hard and answered as she always had. "My mother was widowed before I was born." The statement tasted sour in her mouth. *Oh, why didn't I just burn her papers instead of looking at them? Why did I have to discover that*

44

she lied to me all my life — and taught me to lie as well? "I never knew my father." That much, at least, was the truth.

"I see. What a shame that you have no one."

"Thank you, my lady."

"But I understand Mr. Archer is taking quite a personal interest in you. Such a promising young man, is he not?"

Yes, he makes a lot of promises. But such a glib comment wasn't fair of her. Will seemed to be doing his best for her – and of course for his own benefit as well.

"The heir to an earldom, too. What a nice future he could offer. But I mustn't speculate about his intentions toward you. Young men do so hate to think that women are trying to manage or direct them, or tell them what is expected of them." She looked past Thea as the butler paused in the doorway. "I did think of having just the four of us, but a slightly larger group is so much more amusing, I find. I don't know if that will be true tonight, however, because my other guests are just easing back into society."

That gives me something in common with them – easing into society.

"I thought if you haven't met them yet, you should – given Mr. Archer's position. And what better way than a small, neutral, neighborly gathering? They're just out of mourning, you see."

Thea froze, and the butler said, "Lord and Lady Carrington, my lady."

* * *

Lady Carrington might have been taking the first reluctant steps out of her mourning period, but Will would never have guessed it from the unrelieved black of her high-necked, long sleeved gown. Even the simpler frocks worn by the two young women were far more suited for a party.

She swept a glance across the room, and Will watched in disbelief as she noted and dismissed the companion, eyed Thea with disdain, scowled at him, and finally focused on Lady Stone. "I see you're still indulging your tendency to pick up strays, Lucinda," she snapped.

Lady Stone seemed undisturbed. "Oh, if I wanted strays, Penelope, I'd gather up cats and dogs. The young ladies I acquire as companions or goddaughters are far more entertaining than house pets would be. Have you met Miss Winslow?"

"I've had the pleasure." Lady Carrington's tone made it clear she meant nothing of the sort. "Which category does she fit into? Companion, I suppose?"

"Oh, no. I believe I'll be adopting her as a goddaughter. I'm sure we will have a delightful evening as you get to know her better."

Lady Stone's words were perfectly bland, but Will caught a sparkle in her eyes that was absolutely not the reflection of the fire but of mischief rising within.

"Carrington," she went on, "I'm honored. I'm glad you prevailed upon your lady to come tonight. Such a happy accident that you were in the square this afternoon as Miss Harper and I were taking the air, and that I thought to invite you."

Happy accident? Will was certain it had been no such thing. But what mischief was the woman up to, with this goddaughter business? It seemed Miss Winslow's misgivings about the evening had been far more on target than his own nonchalance.

He cast a sideways glance at Althea and was relieved to see that though she was more pale than usual, she seemed to have herself under tight control. She had risen to make a stiff little curtsy to the older woman, and she seemed unlikely to make any verbal response to the insult Lady Carrington had delivered.

Strays, indeed. Of course, if anything could create a sense of camaraderie between himself and Thea Winslow, that sort of treatment would be a start – lumping them together as lesser beings.

Still, it was going to be a very long evening.

* * *

Thea wished Will Archer would look straight at her, so she could boil him alive with a glare. But he was studiously avoiding her gaze.

Surely, if he'd had any idea of the situation they were walking into, he'd have warned her. Wouldn't he?

After an eternity, the butler announced dinner. Lady Stone claimed Carrington as her escort, and Will Archer very properly offered a bow and his arm to Lady Carrington, who seemed to regard him as somewhat less useful than a wet leaf stuck on her shoe. Thea and Miss Harper, as the lower-ranking females, followed along.

"She's quite something to get used to," the companion offered, her voice low. "Lady Stone, I mean. This is the first time I've encountered Lady Carrington, despite living next door for the entire Season. But she said you two have actually met?"

Thea sighed. Curiosity, it seemed, ran deeply throughout Lady Stone's establishment. "Very briefly. I would not say I know her at all."

Miss Harper raised her eyebrows. "Were I you, I wouldn't be looking forward to a closer acquaintance."

"Or even a neighborly one," Thea agreed as they entered the dining room.

Her first glimpse of the room made it even more clear that Lady Stone's household was unorthodox. Though the finest of white linens and silver gleamed under the glowing chandelier, they were laid on a round table rather than the more traditional rectangular one.

"Is this is a new fashion, Lucinda?" Lady Carrington stiffly took the chair Will held for her.

A bare instant of gratitude for the woman's nosiness flashed through Thea. She'd wondered herself, but she wouldn't have dared to ask.

"Only for households full of women," Lady Stone said lightly. "It is difficult to find enough eligible and unattached gentlemen to fill out a lady's table under any circumstances. But when there's a question of who is to occupy the head of that table... well, you would simply not believe the ideas a male can get into his mind just because a lady asks him to act as host at her party. As though allowing him to occupy that special chair indicates she has an interest in... *ahem*... more."

Thea's gaze met Will Archer's, and for a bare instant she forgot her aggravation with him because the stunned expression in his eyes made her want to giggle. It seemed they were both seeing the same mental vision, of a gray-haired, long-bearded, bent-over old man flirting – or perhaps attempting something far more intimate – with their elderly hostess. Definitely Lady Stone was not the prim and proper stickler for propriety Thea had imagined.

The round table might mean there was no official host, but in other ways the same rules applied. Thea shouldn't have been surprised to find herself seated between Lord Carrington and Miss Harper, and directly across from Lady Carrington. In short, her position couldn't have been more uncomfortable if someone had set it up deliberately. Every time she looked up, the countess's blighting gaze met hers. And with Lord Carrington on her left, she was going to have to talk to him – especially because Lady Carrington seemed bent on ignoring Will, who was seated at her left, in order to monopolize Lady Stone – which meant Will had only Miss Harper to talk to. Not that the companion seemed to mind, for she'd barely spared Thea a glance once everyone had settled at the table. And that left Lord Carrington and Thea.

But perhaps she should look at this as an opportunity to be seized, not an ordeal to endure. At least at dinner – even a somewhat informal one – Lord Carrington couldn't simply ignore her. She might have as much as a couple of hours to convince him that his plan to marry her off to his heir was doomed to failure, and to make the argument that if he gave her a thousand guineas instead, he could be done with the entire problem. But how to begin?

The footman set a dish of creamy soup in front of her.

"I thought my instructions were clear," Lord Carrington said, "that you were to be dressed like a lady. That muddy blue is a bad color for you, too."

At least he wasn't booming out his orders at the top of his

voice. It seemed to Thea that he was trying not to let Lady Carrington overhear. Surely that could be used to her advantage? "I am still in semi-mourning– or had you forgotten about my mother?" She thought better of her tone and tried to sound less challenging. "And these things take time. Even the most skilled modiste cannot turn out an entire wardrobe in a day."

"Then you clearly didn't make it worth her while. Or you don't patronize the right modiste." His gaze flicked over her dress. "Of course, *that* goes without saying."

Thea smiled at him, teeth bared. "Perhaps you will favor me with the name of your favorite one, sir."

He snorted. "Tell your lapdog of a betrothed to hurry up with that special license, and you'll have all the time in the world to get the matter of your wardrobe straightened out. You won't want to wait for a fancy wedding anyway – being in mourning and all."

"I would not leave my situation so lightly." *Or at all.* "I have an obligation to my students, sir, and to my employer."

"What students? Are you a governess somewhere?"

So Will Archer hadn't told him about the school. "Did you think me a lady of leisure? Pray tell, sir, how could I have managed that?"

"You mentioned a teacher's wages, but I thought you meant your mother's."

A slow burn rose in Thea's chest. "I am an adult and perfectly capable, and not so selfish as to remain idle while my mother worked to support us. But perhaps your objection is that you're embarrassed? Indeed, it is true that I might have found employment with a family who are your friends. Or – let me think. Yes, now I have it. You're worried about my safety, because as a governess I might be subjected to an employer who wishes to take advantage." *Just as you did.*

He didn't seem to hear. "Who is your employer?"

Sparring with him was obviously not going to make a dent in his lordship's thick skin. It was just as well that he'd ignored the inference, anyway, because if her intention was to persuade him, attacking his own past behavior was hardly the best approach. "As it happens, sir, you have no worries in that direction. I am a teacher at a girls' school where all the staff are female."

The footman offered the fish course.

Thea helped herself to a morsel she had no intention of eating. "And before you instruct me to resign my position, let me assure you that I plan to remain."

"Married women do not work."

Since he obviously would not understand being devoted to her role, Thea offered a reason he might actually comprehend. "They do if their husbands cannot support them in appropriate style."

"Archer does well enough."

Thea was startled. That was the first hint of approval she had heard him express of anyone, grudging though it was. "Perhaps. Still, without a generous marriage settlement, he could not possibly support me in the way an earl's daughter deserves," she said. *What a prig I sound like.*

But she didn't care what Lord Carrington thought of her, as long as it accomplished the purpose. The more grasping and common she sounded, the more likely he'd realize he wanted nothing more to do with her. And the more likely he'd be to pay her to go away quietly.

"I thought you'd alter your tune, given a little time. And what's your notion of a generous marriage settlement, missy?" For a change, he sounded more curious than bombastic.

In for a penny... "Oh, it would have to be enormous to assure me that marriage to him was worthwhile. And it's not only a matter of money, though of course that's important. You no doubt have several country estates?"

"A few," he admitted.

"At least two of them would need to be settled on your heir, to satisfy me. In different parts of the country, of course, so I can enjoy a change of climate from time to time. Those would need to be outright gifts – not just a matter of giving your permission to live there, since that could be withdrawn at your convenience."

He lifted his wineglass and drank. "Is that all?"

"Oh, no. You must add all the accouterments." She recalled the smooth way Lady Stone's barouche had glided along the streets. She knew little about carriages, but even a novice realized that sort of construction didn't come cheaply. "A proper assortment of carriages, along with the stables to support them. All the servants required to run the various places." She fluttered a hand. "You get the gist, I'm sure. Oh, yes, jewels would not be amiss – especially the family pieces, since Lady Carrington seems unlikely to wear them any time soon. And of course you'd need to sponsor us into the *ton*."

"You want a ticket into society so you will have a place to wear the jewels?" He sounded quite calm.

"Well, it is a shame to leave them locked in a vault. But I'm more concerned that we not be seen as merely the poor relations. You'll need to sponsor Mr. Archer into the best clubs, and see that I am received at all the proper places."

"I am not a duenna, foolish girl. I can't get you vouchers to Almack's."

She let her gaze slide suggestively across the table. "Lady Carrington no doubt could, if you were to suggest it. Oh, and before I forget – of course, we would require a house in town as well. Unless, upon further reflection, you and Lady Carrington would like us to live in Grosvenor Square with you?"

Lord Carrington's gaze flickered. "You do have a way of expressing yourself."

"Or..." Thea let the silence draw out. "Or you could save yourself a whole lot of money and aggravation and explanations. Give me the thousand guineas I require, and you can keep all your other property, not be bothered with your heir being underfoot all the time, not have to explain your past actions to your lady, and never hear from me again."

He laughed. Threw back his head and roared as if she had told the funniest story he'd ever heard.

Everyone at the table stopped talking and turned to stare. Lady Carrington actually dropped her fork; it bounced off her plate to the floor. Will Archer looked a little ill. Lady Stone put her elbow on the table, propped her chin on her fist, and settled in to watch, her beady eyes bright. Thea poked at her fish and wondered what on earth she had said to amuse him so.

"You are an original young woman, I'll give you that." Lord Carrington raised his voice. "Archer, you've got quite the little negotiator here. She's demanded a whole lot more than you've been asking for – and do you know, I'm inclined to give her what she wants. So let's announce the betrothal right now, shall we? – We can finalize the terms tomorrow and have you two married by the end of the week."

* * *

Perhaps it was fortunate that the rules of society meant they had to continue sitting at the table through the rest of an interminable dinner, because it meant Will couldn't act on his intense and – in his view – perfectly reasonable desire to strangle Thea Winslow where she sat.

When the tablecloth was removed and Lady Stone stood to lead the ladies back to the drawing room, she paused beside Will, who had automatically risen when the ladies did, and reached up to lay a hand on his shoulder. He wondered if she meant the gesture to be a comfort or a sort of restraint. "Don't you two sit for long over your brandy," she ordered. "There will be plenty of time tomorrow to finish your discussion of marriage contracts."

She swept out, followed by the other three ladies. Thea lagged a little behind, as if reluctant to leave the two men together.

Will was no more pleased at the idea of a tête-à-tête with his lordship than she apparently was, but having Thea in the room could do nothing but make a bad situation worse. At least this way he could attempt to regain the ground she had lost with whatever wild-hare notion she'd been acting on.

He took his seat again and the butler set the brandy in front of Lord Carrington, who poured a glass for himself and pushed the decanter across the table. "We've plenty to drink to," he said, and raised his snifter. "A toast to your bride."

"Your celebration is a bit premature, sir."

"Oh, nonsense. Quite a woman she is. If I had lingering question about her being mine, this evening would have satisfied any doubts."

Will shot him a warning look and pointedly shifted his gaze to the butler, who had just returned to the room with a box of cigars. The man's face was impassive; he must not have heard.

Lord Carrington seemed not to notice, or to care, that the servant was in the room. "She is precisely what you need, Archer. A namby-pamby sort you are, always willing to see both sides of any question."

Will considered pointing out that it was his profession and not necessarily his nature which led to the sort of balanced perspective which so irritated his lordship. But what was the point of arguing?

Under normal circumstances, he might even have been amused at the aptness of Lord Carrington's observation. He *did* generally see both sides of any question – even this one.

But these were not normal circumstances.

"The earldom can survive a weak man at the helm now and then – it's done so before – but not a whole string of them. She'll not only keep you in line when you step into my shoes, she'll make certain the next generation is up to snuff. With my strong bloodline in them, your boys will be everything I could ask for in my heirs."

Will closed his eyes in pain at the very idea of sons whose personalities resembled this determined old aristocrat. But fretting about something so outlandish, so improbable, was an unnecessary distraction, and right now he could not afford to be drawn away from the point. "Sir, Miss Winslow has given me no reason to think she looks favorably on the idea of marriage to me."

"Well, that goes without saying. But it's not her decision to make, and she'll come around once she realizes the benefits." Carrington chuckled. "She can talk all she wants about demands, but she'll find life a lot more comfortable with those carriages and horses she wants, to say nothing of all the other things on her list."

Will was afraid to hear about *all the other things*. But mostly he was annoyed at the matter-of-fact way Lord Carrington had dismissed him. He seemed to be saying that Thea would eventually adjust to marriage because of the material benefits, despite her prospective husband. The earl seemed to have written Will off as a detriment that could be overcome only by adding more material benefits.

But how foolish of him to take offense at something which was, in the end, meaningless – for all sorts of reasons. Of course, a bride – as well as her family – would consider the material aspects of any potential marriage, for that was the way the world worked. And of course Lord Carrington underestimated and dismissed Will; his opinion of his heir had been firmly set in place six months ago, on their first meeting, and it would not change lightly.

And most important of all, this marriage – no matter how much Lord Carrington wanted it – was simply never going to happen. If there was one thing on the face of the earth that Will Archer and Thea Winslow agreed on, it was that.

Though he couldn't help wondering exactly how many material benefits Lord Carrington believed it would take to mollify both him and Thea.

* * *

At the end of the evening, Lord Carrington offered to call out one of his carriages so Will could escort Thea home. "Might as well give you a glimpse of the quality of my stables," he told Thea. "Not that I'm planning to give you first pick from my own cattle, mind you."

But Lady Stone shook her head. "My guests are my responsibility, Carrington. Though now that the young people are betrothed, at least they won't have to freeze in an open barouche to keep the ton from being scandalized."

The moment the closed carriage pulled away from Grosvenor Square, Thea gathered up her courage. "I'm really sorry. I had no idea things would go so horribly wrong."

Will held up a hand. "Not now. Not till we're away from the square, where no one can possibly hear."

"How could they hear? I'm not planning to scream, you know."

"Well, I may. What in the devil were you doing?"

Thea bit her lip. "I thought if I showed him that the marriage would be ruinously expensive, he would have to change his mind and give up the idea. So I asked for everything I could think of."

"And it seems you thought of a great deal. Not only a country estate, he told me, but servants and stables. I'm surprised you didn't throw in the pack of foxhounds – but then, since you don't ride, why would you care? Plus a house in London, and the jewels. What do you even know about the Carrington jewels?"

"Nothing at all – only I assumed there had to be some. I thought that would be the final straw for him, because even if he agreed to hand those over, Lady Carrington would object."

"In short, you tried to make yourself appear the greediest female on earth."

"Well... yes."

"And you succeeded only too well. Instead of making him back down, you convinced him that you're exactly in tune with him – an offspring worthy of his own greedy heart. How could you not have realized that you were playing straight into his hands?"

"I thought he'd balk at giving up so much money and property."

"And you believed he'd do *what* instead? Pay to save the school? He would never spend money on something that didn't benefit him."

Put that way, her effort sounded very foolish indeed. "I didn't ask him to save the school. I told him I'd just go away."

"If he paid you to disappear."

She nodded. "Lady Carrington would like that, I'm sure."

"He doesn't care what her ladyship wants. *He* doesn't want you to disappear."

"But why?"

"He intends that you shall rescue the earldom."

"From what? I don't know anything about managing estates."

"You're to save it from me." His voice was dry. "By producing sons with the strength and determination to regain any luster or wealth I manage to destroy in my time as earl."

She gulped.

"What did you think he intended to happen by marrying us off? He's said from the very beginning he wants to keep the title in his bloodline."

"I just... didn't think about it, I suppose." *Because I didn't want to think about it.* "Will, I'm really sorry. I've truly messed up everything, haven't I? I really thought such a greedy old man would never give up so much property."

"He obviously doesn't care how expensive something is, when he wants it."

"What are we going to do?"

"*You're* not going to do anything. *I* am going to try to figure out how to regain the ground you lost tonight."

She let the silence draw out. "That's not fair, you know. I was trying my best."

"I know." He sighed. "The truth is I wasn't doing so well either. The few concessions I wrung from him earlier today are nothing compared to your haul, so I shouldn't blame you for making the effort."

"At least I got us a place to live," she said, trying to sound cheerful. "And we could sell the Carrington jewels to save the school – you said there actually *are* jewels?"

"A sapphire and ruby necklace, I believe."

"Red and blue stones in one necklace? Oh, dear, yes, we would definitely sell the jewels."

But her attempt at humor fell flat, and the rest of the ride was quiet.

The carriage drew up on Charlotte Street. Will walked with her to the door of the school, bowed a good night without speaking, and turned back toward the carriage, halting after a few steps. "Wait. Thea?"

She turned, the door half-open behind her. "Yes?"

"What if I can't find a solution?"

"Of course you can. *We* can."

"I mean... would it be so very dreadful?"

"Give in to his demands? You're joking, surely." But he didn't sound as though he was trying to amuse. He seemed to be wondering. Wavering.

What if he were to surrender, leaving her to stand alone? Thea's muscles froze at the thought.

"There would be advantages, you know – for both of us. You said so yourself."

"I said I wanted to wear the Carrington jewels, too," she pointed out acidly. "Go home, Will. Get some sleep. Surely things will look better in the morning."

Chapter Four

But things didn't look better in the morning.

The random sunshine of the last few days had given way to a chilly, dreary, rainy day that felt more like March than mid-May. After her late evening, Thea wanted nothing more than to declare it was still the middle of the night and go back to sleep; the light seeping through her bedroom curtains was tentative enough to make the excuse plausible.

But since that was no way to set an example for the students, she got dressed and went downstairs to where Cook was preparing the morning's porridge for the girls who boarded at the school. "Alice came down earlier, looking for a pail," Cook said. "There's another drip. Right over her bed this time."

Yet another roof leak. And this one must be worse, since water had come all the way through the attic space and into the top-floor servants' rooms – and because the rain today was slow and steady, not the kind of downpour that had caused trouble before.

Thea sighed and climbed the long, narrow flights to help Alice mop up the mess and move her bed. But the room was too small to get the metal frame entirely away from the leaky ceiling. They ended up propping the bucket on the foot of the mattress, which was already thoroughly damp.

"We'll move you down into my room," Thea said.

"Oh, miss, I couldn't put you out like that."

"I'm not letting you sleep in a damp bed. It's no trouble. In fact, I'm doing myself a favor because we can't manage without you if you become ill."

Alice grinned, cheerful again, and went about her regular morning's work.

Thea wished her own mood could be as buoyant. How much would it cost to put a new roof on the school building?

Patching obviously wasn't going to be enough.

When Will had first asked how much money she needed, she'd said a thousand guineas, thinking that would be ample to let them buy the building, make any immediate repairs, and have a nest egg left over to ease future worries. And Will had confirmed her intuition by reacting as though she'd asked for a fortune.

But now it looked as if even that huge sum wouldn't be enough. She'd been joking last night about selling the Carrington jewels, but it might just take that much.

There would be advantages, you know – for both of us.

Marrying her would mean great things for Will, at least. He'd said she had done too good a job with her demands last night, and perhaps he was right. Not because she'd convinced Lord Carrington she was just like him, but because she'd accidentally shown Will how much he stood to gain.

But if she was honest, she had to admit there would be advantages for her as well from this proposed marriage.

Even assuming that some miracle happened and she was able to raise the funds necessary to save the school this time, what would she do if there were to be another crisis? She could never again ask Lord Carrington for help; if she defied him now, she would have burned those bridges beyond any hope of repair.

But if she married Will and they acquired that whole list of property and assets that his lordship seemed to have promised last night, then she could be the school's patron, and Madame would never have to worry again.

Still... marriage was a huge step.

Would it be so very dreadful?

She'd never given much thought to the idea of marrying, because it seemed so far out of the realm for her. A school teacher with a demanding job, a very small income, and little free time had few opportunities to meet eligible men. A young woman with no dowry, no family connections, and no status in society had even fewer.

But to go from her current circumstances to being married off willy-nilly without so much as a by-your-leave...

Yet, if she had to be married at all, Will Archer seemed to be far from the worst possible choice. At least he was young, and clean, and handsome. Intelligent and well-educated. More important, he seemed willing to listen to her, at least some of the time. Unlike Lord Carrington, he didn't dismiss her as a useless appendage, only good for producing sons.

And there was the rub, of course. She rebelled at the very notion of being turned into breeding stock to satisfy his lordship's ideas of nobility and aristocracy, of bloodlines and inheritance and family dynasty.

No, it was impossible.

And yet...

* * *

Thea had been wrong. Things *didn't* look better to Will in the morning.

Lord Carrington listened for less than two minutes before shrugging off Will's comments regarding the agreement made last night at Lady Stone's table. "Just because you weren't involved doesn't make the bargain we struck any less real." His lordship shoved a crumpled list across the desk. "That's all the things she demanded, best I can remember. Now let's turn it into legal language so we can sign it."

Will ran his eye down the page, more to give himself a little time to think than because he was actually studying the list. "The best you can remember?" Surely that meant his lordship's recollection had been convenient, leaving out anything he didn't wish to give up.

Nevertheless, as he deciphered the scrawl, he was impressed not only by Thea's capacity for extortion but by Lord Carrington's memory for details. Everything she'd mentioned to Will last night was there – right down to the Carrington jewels.

He flicked a fingertip against the edge of the paper, trying to gather any possible argument, any feasible objection to the most generous settlement he'd ever heard of, much less executed. "You're certain this is everything she asked for?"

"Down to the last stable boy, pony cart, and earbob. Check it with her if you must, but it's all there – I know better than to give her an excuse to back out now."

How very cunning of him to agree. If he'd held back on a single detail, Will could have stood firm and at least delayed the process. But he hadn't.

"Probably just as well she took over the negotiations," Carrington observed. "Since you're technically my solicitor, it wouldn't look right if you were the one sticking me up like a highwayman." There was a note in his voice that was almost pride.

Will considered that angle as a potential delaying tactic. What if, as Lord Carrington's own solicitor, he objected that the settlement was too generous? That it was unfair to his client? *That would get you laughed out of the room.*

Carrington poured himself a glass of port, lit a cigar, and eyed his heir narrowly. "What's the problem, boy? What more can you possibly want? You can be a rich man within days, instead of waiting around for me to give up the ghost. What do you have to kick about?"

And how was he supposed to answer that? *I want a seat in Parliament?* – the old man could no doubt come up with that as well.

If he had been setting out to negotiate a marriage settlement for one of his clients, Will would never have dared to propose the sort of terms Thea seemed to have rattled off the top of her head last night. But now that she'd laid out her demands, there was literally nothing else he could ask for. As ridiculous as it sounded, if she had tried to hamstring his power to negotiate, she couldn't have done a better job.

"Besides," Carrington went on, "she's a pretty girl. It should be no hardship for you to take her to bed."

The old man was crude, but he wasn't exactly wrong – about any of it. The generosity of the proposed settlement. The effect the agreement would have on Will's life. And especially about Thea being attractive.

That creamy, delicate, no doubt soft skin. The way the red highlights in her chestnut hair gleamed in the sun. The wide, clear brown eyes that he hadn't – until just this minute – even remembered that he had noticed.

At least, Will would have thought her very attractive if he hadn't found himself skewered by that sharp tongue of hers far too often for comfort. No, pretty though she was, Thea Winslow was not what he was looking for in a wife.

But how often did men in his position truly get to choose?

Before Robert's death, when he had still been just plain Will Archer, Esquire, he'd given little thought to marriage. Living in chambers and working to establish himself in a career left little time for social pursuits. Even if there had been a young woman who captured his attention, marriage would have to wait until he was in better financial circumstances.

Then Robert died, and suddenly Will was the heir to an earldom. But the spot he found himself in would be even more difficult. Society's expectations of him had risen; he could no longer choose just any young woman, he must find one worthy of being a countess one day. One who could win Lord Carrington's approval, or else was so wealthy in her own right that whether Carrington left him anything beyond the title wouldn't matter.

But the father of any eligible young woman of the *ton* would take one look at him and see a man who was tied to a time-consuming career, with no assurance that he'd ever be better off despite being the presumptive heir to a cantankerous old peer. Any father in that position would refuse to consider him a worthy match for any young woman of breeding or fortune.

He'd understood early on that he would face a dilemma when the time came to marry, but he'd been too busy to put much thought into the matter.

And then Thea Winslow had come along.

He realized his thoughts had drifted far away from the bookroom, and pulled himself back. What was Lord Carrington rattling about?

"Not that I'm going to be a fool about it," the old man said. "Take the London house, for instance. Don't come back here saying you've bought the most expensive place in town, wanting me to hand over unlimited gold to pay for it. I'll agree to a sum, and if the place she wants costs more than that, you can find the rest somewhere else."

"That seems fair."

"As for giving you two estates in the country..."

"*Two*?" Will's voice cracked.

"What's the matter, boy? Think that's more than you can handle?"

Will wouldn't have admitted it aloud, but for the first time in six months he found himself in complete agreement with Lord Carrington. What had Thea been thinking?

Still, a good negotiator never conceded too quickly. "Managing a country place – or two – will be good practice for later on," he said, trying to keep his voice level.

"You're not fooling me, young man. If you don't want them, just tell the girl she'll have to do without." There was a malicious sparkle in Carrington's eyes. "Of course if she balks, it won't be my fault."

Will's head throbbed. "I believe that on further consideration, Thea will agree that two households – one in London, one in the country – will be plenty for now."

"You *believe*? Be careful you don't end up living under the cat's paw, letting her run roughshod over you."

"I should think that's exactly what you would like, sir – Miss Winslow making the decisions."

"She's been doing all right for herself so far. Tell you what, Archer. Get her with child inside a year and there's five thousand guineas for you – ten if it's a boy – and she can have her second country place. That doesn't need to be in the contract, of course. Just an agreement between gentlemen."

"I would not under any circumstances enter into such a bargain, sir."

"Why not?" His lordship relit his cigar and looked Will over speculatively. "Surely you're enough of a man to enjoy that challenge."

Heat swept over Will – caused by anger, of course. Fully-justified anger, not at the insult to him but at the idea of

Carrington speaking about Thea that way. "Sir, I must ask you to treat Miss Winslow with the respect that is due her."

"Or what?" Carrington's eyes narrowed. "Imagine that. It turns out you have a spine after all. Interesting that it only seems to appear when the subject is this girl." He puffed the cigar. "Time to stop dancing around and make up your mind, Archer. I'm losing my patience."

And that, Will thought, would be the first evidence that Lord Carrington had ever possessed any.

"Take the deal or leave it– *today*."

"I can't do that, sir. Not without discussing it with Thea. Miss Winslow."

"Then tomorrow. But no later. And while you're *discussing* it with my daughter, make sure she understands she's pushed me just as far as she can. She won't like what will happen to both of you if this marriage doesn't come off."

There was nothing more to say after that. Will excused himself, took his hat and stick from Jenkins at the front door, and walked unsteadily out into Grosvenor Square.

* * *

Thea spent a good deal of the morning in the dining room, teaching her class of young ladies how to properly lay a table – and overriding the objection by one of them that she didn't need the lesson.

"I already know how to use all the knives and forks when I'm eating," she said, "and as for the rest, that's what housekeepers and butlers and footmen are for."

"But how will you know if they've done it properly?" Thea asked sweetly. "If they don't, you'll be embarrassed before your grand friends who do know the correct way."

Before the girl could argue further, Alice poked her head into the room and beckoned wildly at Thea.

She sighed and went to the door.

"Mr. Archer's here, miss," Alice whispered. "He refused to wait in the rain, so he just walked in. I put him in Madame's sitting room."

Thea blinked. No wonder Alice had tried to stay quiet. Not only had she allowed a forbidden man onto the premises, but she'd put him in Madame's own room. "I'll get him out before the girls can get wind of a visitor. And for your sake, don't mention this to Madame, please – I'll tell her later and make sure she doesn't blame you."

"That's just it, miss. Madame's there."

Thea closed her eyes against the sudden pain in her temples. "Very well." She told the girls to each set a place at the big table, using all the rules they'd reviewed, and put the eldest of them in charge. "I'll be back in a few minutes. Use your time well."

She paused by the hallway mirror to give an unnecessary touch-up to her hair and tapped on the half-open door of Madame's sitting room.

Will leaped to his feet, and Madame said, "There you are, Thea. Mr. Archer has been kind enough to keep me company while we waited for Alice to find you. Imagine my surprise to find that he's been calling on you."

"I'm so sorry, Madame. I – We'll go."

"Out in the rain? Don't be foolish. I've ordered tea. Do sit down, Thea, so that Mr. Archer can be comfortable."

He didn't look comfortable. He looked miserable.

Thea wondered how much he'd told Madame, and under what duress. But even a headmistress who could wring the truth out of a reluctant schoolgirl in under a minute couldn't have the same success with a solicitor who was practiced in keeping secrets – could she?

Thea sat, and Alice came in with the tea tray. Madame filled a cup and passed it across the low table to Will. "Do try the lemon tarts. Cook does a particularly good job with them." She poured Thea's tea. "Since it appears you two have something to discuss, I shall go and supervise your class, Thea. Is it dining room manners, today?"

"Table-setting. Thank you, Madame."

Will rose as Madame did, and stood silently until she had gone. "Shall I close the door?"

"No, it wasn't accidental that she left it ajar."

"To keep you from screaming at me?"

"To protect my reputation. Why? Am I going to want to scream at you?"

"Most likely." He sat down again, shifting his feet on the faded Oriental rug as though he was trying to get comfortable.

"Your negotiations didn't take long this morning."

"His lordship declared there was nothing else to negotiate, and he handed me this list."

She took it warily. "What's this?"

"He said it's everything you asked for. Well, except for the second estate – we agreed that you were overreaching there. It's to be turned into a legally-binding document, and he wants our agreement by tomorrow." He sighed. "Or else."

Thea glanced at the paper, but she didn't really see the scrawl. "I truly made a muddle of things, didn't I?"

He didn't answer, only took a deep breath. She stole a look at him, trying to brace herself for the explosion. At the least, he'd surely make clear the many ways in which she had fallen short, interfered, meddled...

"You had the best of intentions," he said.

Tears prickled, and she blinked them back. She didn't deserve for him to be gentle; she knew how very badly she had erred. She hadn't caused the situation they were caught in, but she had definitely made it worse.

She had never missed her mother more than she did right now. What would Anna have said? She had been, if nothing else, pragmatic. But would she have advised Thea to surrender, or to hold her head high and defy Lord Carrington's threats? Accept a known, if unpleasant, course of action, or take a chance that the alternative wouldn't be worse?

"Madame doesn't seem such a bad sort," Will said. "Breaking her rules to let me come in out of the rain. Offering tea. Giving us a little privacy for our discussion."

"Don't assume she's impressed with you. That's her way – rigidly perfect manners, no matter who she's dealing with. She's curious, that's all, because I haven't told her about you. I mean, about any of this." She picked up her tea, but her hand trembled and the cup rattled so loudly against the saucer that she quickly set it back down.

The alternative, she thought, could be so very much worse.

"I've been thinking, Will, about what you said." Her voice felt a little sticky. "How maybe it wouldn't be so very dreadful. Perhaps you're right."

She thought for a moment that he wasn't going to answer. "We haven't much of a choice."

Not the sort of excited response a young woman wished to hear when she'd just accepted an offer of marriage, Thea thought dryly. But then she hadn't been very enthusiastic herself.

Of course, the majority of marriages in the *ton* were probably no different. Straightforward business deals, agreed to because of families and money and property and society, and not particularly welcomed by the people at the center of the bargain. At least she and Will were being honest with each other.

"I thought about asking Lady Stone for help," Will said, his voice low. "She likes you, that was clear, and I thought perhaps she could think of something I hadn't. She might agree to take you under her wing."

"What would that accomplish?"

"If she were to announce that she knows and accepts your family and your origins, then anything Lord Carrington said about you would be dismissed."

"Then he wouldn't be able to carry out his threat to marry me off to someone..." She didn't want to say *Someone even worse than you.*

But it was clear he understood what she'd been thinking. "I believe she's unconventional enough that she might do it. She does seem to have an unnatural number of so-called goddaughters. But—"

"You didn't talk to her?"

Will shook his head. "I can't ask her to dabble in potential scandal without being honest about your situation. We'd have to tell her exactly why Carrington thinks he has the right to dictate your marriage."

"And if she didn't take it well, and she breathed even a word..." Thea shivered. "I don't think it would help much anyway, because it wouldn't save the school. And I'm not convinced it would stop Lord Carrington either, since he doesn't seem to give the flick of a finger for scandal."

"And being challenged might only make him more determined to have his way."

She picked up the teapot. "I know you're just as unhappy about this as I am, Will, but it appears that we're stuck with each other."

He frowned a little.

She refilled his cup. "Once that contract is signed, you're certain he can't back out of any of it?"

"I'm sure. I'm quite capable in my profession, Thea."

"Sorry, I didn't mean to say you weren't. The wedding won't actually happen till after he signs?"

"Well – I doubt he'll agree to sign in advance, any more than we'd agree to go through the vows before he has legally committed himself. But I'll stipulate that everything has to be done on the day of the wedding, at the same time. He signs the contract and executes the deeds – all while the bishop looks on as a witness, ready to conduct the wedding ceremony."

"If he can't change his mind, it doesn't have to be a real marriage." She saw the doubt in his face. "Oh, it will be legal, of course. But not a *marriage*, just an alliance. An... *a convenient marriage*, I think it's called."

"You mean an unconsummated marriage," Will said slowly.

"Well – yes." She felt heat rise in her face. "I mean, it's not like there's any sort of attraction between us. Given the right situations, we might be friends, but this is just a business deal. Anyway, marriage – everything that goes along with marriage – has never been something I expected. I assumed I'd be a spinster schoolteacher, like Madame. And like my mother, really. Even though she had me, she never considered another..." She was babbling, but she couldn't seem to stop herself. "Now, of course, I understand why in my whole life she never showed interest in any man. But because of the way I was raised, the path I've taken, it has never occurred to me to think of being a wuh…" Even saying the word was difficult. "A wife."

Mercifully, Will intervened. "I understand why you're reluctant."

"Then you agree?"

He paused, and the silence stretched out uncomfortably. "I think what you're asking is fair. For now."

Thea frowned at the caveat. How long was *for now*, anyway? Years? Months? Weeks? Minutes? Would he keep his promise at all, or was it just a way to smooth things over till the deed was done and it was too late for her to change her mind? The moment the ring was on her finger, a woman became her husband's property.

Could she trust Will not to go back on his word? *For now* wasn't actually much of a promise. Would he be insulted if she asked him to put this agreement in writing? Surely not, for he had insisted that Lord Carrington agree to a written contract. But if he thought she was doubting his word as a gentleman…

He had listened to her. Had said he understood. Had treated her as an equal.

He might be feeling the same kind of relief she did just now, if he too would prefer a partnership rather than a more traditional marriage. It wasn't as though either of them had a romantic view of the situation. And it wasn't as though he *wanted* to marry her, any more than she wanted to marry him.

"And we won't be spending much time together anyway," she went on firmly. "You have your career, and I'll be at the school. At least – we *are* going to save the school, aren't we?"

He seemed to see the question in her eyes. "Yes, Thea. We'll save the school."

The knot which had taken hold inside her days ago – the knot she had tried to pretend didn't exist – relaxed just a little. Yes, she *could* trust him; Will would keep the promises he'd made. "Then I suppose the only remaining question is, when's the wedding?"

No – there were two remaining questions. How was she possibly going to explain all this to Madame?

* * *

Lord Carrington read the preliminary draft Will had brought to their appointment with disdain and irritation. "I said I wanted this finished," he fumed, and Will was surprised only that his lordship didn't lose his temper outright.

"Actually turning a scrawled list of terms into a legal contract does take a certain amount of time," Will pointed out. "It's only sensible to look at each section and work out any small changes in the language so the entire contract doesn't need to be copied over and over."

"That's what clerks are for." Lord Carrington scowled. "You needn't think I'm paying you for this delay. If you're totting up a bill based on the number of days you're taking to write a simple agreement, you'll find yourself out of sorts."

Considering that Lord Carrington had yet to pay him a single shilling for any of his work, that was hardly a shock. And there was no benefit to pointing out that this was far from a simple agreement. "I would not dream of sending you my account, sir."

"Damn foolish of you not to."

Will blinked. "But you just said—"

"I said I wasn't going to pay for all this delay. But if you're doing work for free, that's just another example of why you'd never get ahead on your own. Good thing my girl will keep you straight."

"Do you even remember *your girl's* name, sir?"

His lordship glared. "Eventually, when I'm dead and gone, it'll be Carrington – and that's the only thing I care about. Now let's get down to business."

Working out details – and sometimes arguing over the difference between one word and another – took hours. By the time they stopped for the day, Will was exhausted. Lord Carrington, by contrast, seemed energized by the battle. *But then he isn't the one who stayed up all night drafting the damn thing.*

Will stood on the stoop outside the Carrington house for a few minutes, simply enjoying being able to breathe freely as he braced himself to head back to his desk at Lincoln's Inn for what would no doubt be another long night's work.

Just down the street, Lady Stone's front door opened and she appeared, wearing the most outlandish hat he'd seen in years. The thing was huge, and piled with what looked like fruit and flowers.

Coincidence, he told himself. She couldn't possibly have been lying in wait for him to appear; she'd have had to be hovering by a window, already dressed to go out, watching for him – and he was hardly that important in Lady Stone's world.

She did look pleased to see him, though. She paused on her stoop and waved an imperious hand to summon him. "Dear boy, I'm on my way to call on your young lady now."

Will made a show of looking up and down the street. He saw a dray hauling barrels, a groom holding a pair of handsome grays who were hitched to a racing curricle, a hansom cab which had just picked up a fare, and a wagon full of what looked like masonry tools – but there was no crested barouche to be seen. "Without your carriage?" he said sweetly.

"Of course I've ordered my carriage, but I want a stroll first. And since I just happened to see you, I thought what fun it would be if I was escorted on my walk by a handsome young man. How are the Carringtons today?" She took his arm.

A short stroll sounded inviting – a nice break before plunging once more into details and minutia – even if he had to maintain a firm guard on his tongue. "Since I did not see her ladyship, I cannot report. But his lordship is in fine health."

"In other words, he's being irritable and difficult as usual. Tell me, what are your plans?"

"Plans, my lady? To walk with you, and then work all night if necessary on Lord Carrington's business."

"Those are not the kind of plans I'm interested in. Where's the wedding to be? St. George's, Hanover Square? Or will you ask the bishop for a special license? Oh, yes, that's more likely, since your bride is still technically in mourning for her mother. And surely the happy day will not be long delayed?"

"It would hardly be polite of me to tell you the details before Miss Winslow knows them."

Her contemplative silence made him uneasy.

"So you and his lordship have worked it all out between you?" she said finally. "How interesting. One has to wonder why Carrington feels so very invested in your wedding, Mr. Archer. Or is it Miss Winslow he's most interested in getting settled?"

Will felt his breath catch. He really was off his game today, to underestimate the most notorious gossip he'd ever met. "Of course he has an interest in his heir's future…"

She tipped her head so she could look up at him from under the wide brim of the hat, her eyes beady and inquisitive, and shook her head sadly, as though disappointed by his effort.

He tried again. "I'm only thinking of your comfort, my lady. If I told you, it would be difficult for you not to let something slip when you're talking to Miss Winslow. And you wouldn't want her to feel like the last to know."

She laughed. "You're a complete hand, young man. Very well – I'll find out some other way. Perhaps I should invite the bishop to dinner." She paused. "Oh, bother. I should have turned the other direction."

Will looked up to see a large man coming toward them, raising his hat.

The hat was clearly expensive, as was the blue broadcloth coat and the shining boots, but somehow though each piece was right, the man didn't present quite the polished whole he'd no doubt aimed for. "My lady. I was hoping to talk to you again." The words were carefully enunciated, as if he'd practiced, but there was a hint of an accent underlying them. Cockney? No, not that – but something similar.

"Mr. Tomlinson," Lady Stone said coolly. "When do you anticipate the work on my chimneys being completed?"

Ah, Will thought. *The builder is still be making a nuisance of himself.*

"Should be tomorrow, my lady. That's why I'm here now, to check on the workers. This would be the time to add those parapets we talked about, while the men are already on site, you know. Have you thought it over?"

"I do not need parapets. I am – as I told you days ago – only interested in the chimneys."

"They would look right good, though," Mr. Tomlinson argued.

"You are not going to talk me into doing work that doesn't need to be done, Mr. Tomlinson. Finish the job, send in your bill, and move on."

"Only offering you an opportunity, my lady. Less expensive to build while we're up there than it will be to come back. But it's up to you, of course. You know where to find me. Inside or out, up or down – you want it, I'll build it." He sniffed thoughtfully. "Or tear it down, come to that. It's all the same to me."

Will asked idly, "Do you happen to mend roofs?"

"Does a cat lick its whiskers? What kind of a roof?"

"Do you mean what materials, or what sort of building?"

Lady Stone tapped her foot. "*Mr. Archer.*"

"Yes, ma'am." Will extracted a calling card from his briefcase. "Perhaps you can stop by my chambers so we can discuss the matter."

The builder eyed the card, and then stared at Will. "Archer? You're something to do with that lord next door, aren't you?"

"I had no idea," Lady Stone said acidly, "that you were such a close follower of Burke's Peerage, Mr. Tomlinson."

"Well, if it's his roof you mean, I've already tried to talk to him about it. It's nothing major, just some loose tiles my men noticed – but he wouldn't even let me inside to talk. Quite a tartar, that fella, from what I've heard."

"From what you've *heard*?" A lesser man would have quailed under Lady Stone's tone. "In this neighborhood? Surely you don't mean from *my* servants?"

"I hear things wherever I go, my lady, and my job takes me all around. People are the most frightful tongue-waggers, you know. They ought to be ashamed of themselves, but there you have it." Tomlinson bowed and walked away.

Sauce for the goose, Will thought, and bit his lip hard to keep from laughing at the expression on Lady Stone's face at the very idea that *her* servants might have indulged in such a horrid thing as gossip.

Chapter Five

The day after the dinner party, Thea used the occasion as a lesson for her etiquette class, requiring each of the young ladies to imagine the party and then write an appropriate thank-you letter to their hostess. Her plan was to take advantage of the time they spent in quiet scratching of pens on paper to compose her own note to Lady Stone. The students' assignment was quite simple compared to her own, however, because how did one cordially thank a hostess who had – even if innocently – helped to set off the most calamitous cascade of events in one's life?

She had to make several attempts, and by the time she was satisfied, she had ruined more notepaper than she liked to think about. But eventually she managed a polite missive and dispatched it via a boy who ran errands in the neighborhood, paying him a shilling from her meager reserves to be sure it was promptly delivered.

Then she put the matter out of her mind, for that would no doubt be the end of it. Lady Stone had satisfied her curiosity, and after the way her party had turned into disaster, she would surely never want to hear Thea Winslow's name again.

So she was taken aback the day after her note had been sent off when she joined Madame for their regular conference over afternoon tea and found three visitors filling the sitting room to the brim. They hadn't just arrived, either, because Lady Stone was chatting comfortably with Madame as she sipped her tea. Miss Harper had obviously been asked to pour, for she was just handing a cup and saucer to Will when Thea came in.

Startled though she was to see the ladies, Thea's gaze was instantly focused on Will. She'd been half-expecting he would come to report, and half-hoping that if he didn't, it was because there had been no progress. Silly, of course, to wish for more delays, when the important decisions had already been made and the school itself was hanging in the balance. If they were going to marry, they might as well get on with it. At least they could secure the necessary funds so that *something* could end up as she had hoped.

He looked serious, thoughtful, sober... She wondered if that meant there were more roadblocks, or if their path had been cleared, leaving him feeling just as many doubts, just as much hesitation, as she was.

"Thea," Madame said, "you have callers."

Thea's cheeks felt hot. How gauche of her to simply stand there and stare, rather than make her curtsy.

"Oh, don't fret the girl," Lady Stone said. "It's clear they have eyes only for each other. These young couples in love never seem to realize anyone else is in the room, so the rest of us may as well be amused by their antics."

Thea blinked at that. *Antics?* Yes, she had been staring at Will, but... in love? *Old women can be very silly sometimes.* "My lady, how nice of you to visit. My apologies, I should have greeted you and Miss Harper immediately."

"Heavens, child, I'm quite well entertained by becoming acquainted with Madame. Mr. Archer, do take Thea away so you can talk to her. I know you're intent on getting back to your business without delay."

Will glanced at the clock on Madame's mantel and set his cup down. "I just need a moment, Thea. Will you walk me out?"

He wasn't staying? Her heart seemed to sag. But of course she only cared because she had gotten her hopes up, thinking that he might have brought news. *Real* news, not the sort that could be exchanged along with a simple goodbye that anyone might observe.

As they walked through the building to the front door, she tried to ignore the lineup of girls' faces staring intently down the staircase.

"The lessons in deportment do not seem to be going well," Will murmured.

She shot an irritated look up at him. "There have been

extra challenges lately, and many additional temptations for them with all this coming and going."

"How delightful of you to consider me a temptation."

Had she *really* said he was tempting? She supposed it was true enough – at least in the view of the girls. A real gentleman, well-dressed, well-mannered, handsome... A young woman could do far worse than to take Will Archer as an example of what a gentleman should be. It was really no wonder the girls hung out of the windows and over the stair rail to get a look.

And if she was honest, it wasn't just the girls who had noticed. Thea had to admit the man had some sort of magnetic ability to draw her attention. For just an instant, when she had first come into Madame's sitting room, she hadn't even really seen Lady Stone or Miss Harper; her attention had landed instantly and inevitably on Will. He had commanded the room even though he was only standing there, reaching for the cup Miss Harper held out. He had done nothing to draw her notice, but still she had forgotten her manners, passed over the ladies, to focus on him.

The idea of being drawn to him like that made her feel nervous and ill at ease. Maybe it was his scent. Not quite sweet, not quite smoky, absolutely not flowery, not quite *anything* she could put her finger on, but it was very pleasant nonetheless.

Fortunately the girls weren't going to get close enough to smell the man, so at least they would be safe from the temptation Thea felt to bury her nose in his coat – or perhaps in his neck – and try to find the source of that alluring scent.

She shook off the nonsensical thought. "If you have no particular news for me, why are you here?"

"You'll find that Lady Stone is nearly as good at getting her own way as Lord Carrington is."

"That's not an answer. In fact, it sounds more like a warning."

"Only if you don't want to go shopping, I suppose. And I'm here because I'm on my way back to chambers and her ladyship offered transport to save me a jolting ride in a hansom or an exhaustingly-long walk. Her words, not mine."

Then he hadn't intended to come to visit her at all? Maybe he hadn't even wanted to come. How foolish of her to feel just a bit disappointed.

He looked searchingly down at her. "His lordship and I made considerable progress today. The contract should be completed in another day, ready for the final copies to be made."

"What is there left to argue about?"

"Mostly details, but Lord Carrington is absolutely dogged when it comes to hashing things out – like which country estate to hand over."

She blinked. "You mean he actually agreed to *one*?"

"A smallish manor house, with property, in Surrey. It's reasonably close to London, and I thought you'd prefer it to the other choice."

"Why? Was there something wrong with the other one?"

"It's located practically next door to Monkscroft. I thought it was a bit too close to be comfortable." He took a deep breath. "He's determined to hold the wedding on Wednesday morning, in Grosvenor Square. He told me he would send word to the bishop this afternoon to make the appointment."

It was no more than Thea had expected, but she braced herself against the shock that her life was about to change so dramatically... only to feel no jolt at all. Perhaps she had already adapted, for there was only a bone-deep sense of inevitability.

"Wednesday's not the best day," she said. "My classes..."

"But no other day will be any better."

"I suppose that's true. If it must be Wednesday, then it must."

"I'd better get back to work so everything is ready." Will took his hat from the stand and let himself out. Thea watched him walk over to speak to the coachman, still sitting in the barouche which stood in front of the school, before he climbed in and the carriage clattered off down Charlotte Street.

He was headed for his chambers, he had said. She was glad to see that he wasn't walking the rest of the way. He looked so tired that she had wanted to soothe him, to take him back to the sitting room and make him drink his tea and eat every sandwich and tart on the cakestand, to rest a while.

"You're growing positively maudlin," she muttered to herself, and went back to Madame's sitting room.

Lady Stone's eyes were particularly bright and beady. "I was just telling Madame that your new role in society will require a much different wardrobe."

Madame looked quizzically at Thea.

"What I already have will be perfectly adequate, my lady."

"Nonsense, my girl. I am certain, however, that you'd rather do these things quietly, so I'll summon my own modiste to Grosvenor Square. That way we can make our selections in leisure. When will be a good time for you to come? I'm sure we shouldn't delay long, if you're to have a dress ready for your wedding by...." She paused delicately and lifted her eyebrows.

Thea felt mesmerized by those beady, all-knowing eyes. "Wednesday."

A tiny hiss escaped from Madame – the most out-of-control reaction Thea had ever seen her display.

"Then we must act tomorrow. I will send the carriage for you at nine." Lady Stone stood up, brushing her hands down the lace panel that trimmed the front of her skirt. "Come, Miss Harper – you have an immense amount of work to do before then."

After Thea saw the ladies to the door, walked them to the barouche, and said her farewells, she reluctantly returned to the sitting room.

The silence was heavy, broken only by the click of Madame's cup against her saucer. Thea sat down, feeling weary and dreading the reckoning to come.

"You told me that Mr. Archer was Lord Carrington's solicitor and he was trying to arrange funds to purchase the school."

"That's all quite true," Thea said quietly.

"You did not see fit to mention that Mr. Archer is Lord Carrington's heir, next in line to the title. Or that you're planning to marry him."

"I was hoping it wouldn't come to... I mean... it was only decided for certain yesterday. You and I were both busy with late classes and then dinner, and there hasn't really been an opportunity to talk privately. I intended to tell you today, over tea."

"Thea, what have you *done*?"

Thea nibbled at her fingertip. She should have known that waiting, trying to find a way to ease into this conversation, would only cause more trouble in the end. She couldn't bear it if Madame felt that Thea had sacrificed herself to save the school. And Madame was capable of refusing help that came at such a personal cost.

So her course was clear. She would simply have to lie.

"I know it's a shock, Madame. I found it so myself, for I never considered that marriage would be possible for me. And then to have simply stumbled on a man like Will – and I don't think I've told you, but that's literally what happened. I tripped on Lord Carrington's front stoop, and Will saved me from a dreadful fall. I realize you don't know him as well as I do, but he truly is thoughtful, kind, and gentle, and so easy to talk to."

"That," Madame said tartly, "I can well believe. I myself have been tempted to tell him... but that's not the point just now. A wedding on *Wednesday*? You'll have known him less than a fortnight!"

Thea shrugged. "There are society couples who have never met before the wedding ceremony."

"That is hardly a standard to emulate!"

"I'm of age, Madame," Thea said quietly.

Madame closed her eyes, and Thea thought she seemed to grow older as the moments passed. She hadn't realized, somehow, that her own growing-up years meant that Madame was no longer a young woman.

"What would your mother say?" Madame murmured.

"I hope she would wish me happy." Thea sat down on the arm of Madame's chair – a familiarity she hadn't been allowed since she was a child – and put an arm gently around the woman. "This is what I want. I want marriage. I want a–" Her voice cracked. "I want a family."

If lying means going to hell, I might as well get used to flames.

But she found lying got easier as she went along, for she sounded firm and steady and very sure of herself when she said, "I want Will."

"But this unseemly haste..." Madame cleared her throat. "It's not that I object to your choice, Thea. He seems a pleasant young man, and with his profession you will never need to worry. Also, I must say I suspected the wind was blowing in that direction. At least I hoped you were not being careless with your reputation with that young man, and also that neither of you was toying with the other's affections. For it is clear to me that you both feel affection."

If teaching doesn't work out, I could try the stage. I seem to have a talent for acting.

"But what on earth is the hurry? Surely this young man will wait so that you can be certain."

What sort of reasoning would Madame find acceptable, to justify the haste?

"Lord Carrington wants to see his heir married," she said finally.

Madame's gaze sharpened. "And married... to you? I think I see. No matter what I say, I will not change your mind, I gather."

"No, Madame."

"Then I can only hope that this young man's character, and your feelings about him, are truly as strong as you believe they are. Bring him to see me again, Thea. I wish to get to know him better, since he will be so very important to you – and since you are the closest thing to a daughter I will ever know."

Thea nodded and told herself that even deception was forgivable when it was for a good cause.

She hoped Will would be as convincing at deceiving Madame. But she wasn't looking forward to telling him that he would have to pretend to have fallen in love with her.

* * *

When Will arrived in Grosvenor Square for what he hoped would be his final daily meeting with Lord Carrington, he was not surprised to see Lady Stone's barouche pulling up in front of her house – except that he wouldn't have thought her ladyship to be such an early riser. Then the footman ran to open the carriage door and help Thea down.

The morning was bright and warmer than the last week had been, and she was dressed for spring, wearing a fitted spencer over her dark gray walking dress, with a hat instead of the plain bonnet she'd generally worn.

He strolled over to meet her on the pavement. "Has her ladyship convinced you to go shopping?"

"It seems when you are at the highest levels of society, you do not need to go anywhere. Shopping comes to you."

"That's handy. I'll keep it in mind."

"I am glad to encounter you this morning, because–"

That's a first. It was a pleasant sensation, too; far nicer to have his prospective wife be happy to see him, rather than go running in the other direction. But she didn't look pleased; she looked wary, tentative. Even guilty. *What have you done now, Thea?*

"Madame wishes you to call on her. I know you're very busy and this is just another obligation to fit in, when you already have so many. But if you could visit, it would help to allay her fears. She's worried about how quickly this is all happening."

"I'll find time," Will assured her. "It's only natural that she feels an obligation to ask the sort of questions that your mother would."

"And if you could convince her–" She took a deep breath.

Will noticed with appreciation that she seemed to have been hiding quite a good figure under those demure dresses.

The footman returned. "Your pardon, sir, miss. Lady Stone's compliments, sir, and would you accompany the young lady inside for a few minutes, please?"

Will offered his arm to Thea and said warily, "Convince Madame of what?"

Thea shot a look at the footman and whispered, "That we took just one look at each other and fell in love."

He stared at her in shock, but there was no time for more. The footman swung the front door open and the butler was waiting to take them upstairs to Lady Stone's sitting room, where her ladyship and Miss Harper were already looking at bolts of fabric.

Lady Stone wheeled around and came toward the door. "No, Mr. Archer, don't come in, for we can't possibly let you see anything that might become your bride's wedding dress. But I only need a few minutes of your time anyway. I'm assuming you're not planning to take an immediate honeymoon journey?"

Thea looked startled by the notion, and her gaze – full of suspicion – flickered to Will's face.

Convince her that we took one look at each other and fell in love...

Thea had been talking about Madame and not Lady Stone, but he might as well practice looking and sounding like a lovelorn bridegroom – and best to do it before her ladyship noticed that the bride looked anything but pleased at the idea of a wedding journey. "Regrettably, no, my lady. The press of my business requires me to stay in town for now, but we'll spend the summer at our estate in Surrey."

Thea emitted a little squeak of protest, and Will's fingers tightened on her arm in warning.

Lady Stone frowned. "I wasn't aware you had property. And isn't Carrington's seat in Hampshire?"

"It is, my lady, but his lordship is providing us with a country home as a wedding gift."

"Is he, now?" She looked intrigued. "I never thought of him as so generous. Well, that's neither here nor there. My last ball of the season is to be held on Thursday. It can serve as your introduction to the *ton*, Thea – and of course yours too, Mr. Archer, since you've also been in mourning."

"A ball?" Thea's voice was small. "Oh, please, Lady Stone – no. I was only joking when I told Lord Carrington I wanted to enter into society."

"Nonsense, child. Yours is an interesting story – both of you coming out of nowhere – and now it's a romantic one as well. If Society doesn't get a good look at you both soon, you'll become a subject for speculation, with everyone wondering whether there's something odd about you."

She made an excellent point. Will knew the only reason he hadn't already been subjected to pressure from the matchmaking mamas of the *ton* – at least the ones who didn't entirely comprehend his uncertain position – was that the official mourning period after Robert's death had so neatly overlapped the Season. To turn up with an unknown wife, but then not to appear in public, would be cause for comment among the cream of society. Lady Stone might be the most notorious gossip in London, but she was far from the only one.

"Yes," her ladyship mused. "I think doing it this way will create much less pressure than if the ball were actually to be in your honor. Not that I wouldn't be delighted to host a ball just for you, and I claim the right to do so next Season – especially since I'm quite certain Penelope Carrington will never think of doing such a thing."

Will's heart sank. *We're going to have to tell her the truth.*

It was one thing to attend a ball as part of a crowd, as just two more names on an extensive list. But to be her guests of honor meant Lady Stone would be vouching for them both, linking their reputations to hers – and if any scandal were to cling to them, it would blast her as well. Fortunately they had a little time before it would be necessary to confide every last detail.

Thea was still scrambling for excuses to dodge the upcoming party. "I wouldn't want to embarrass you, my lady. I have nothing to wear that's suitable."

Lady Stone waved a hand. "I'm sure we'll find something in this mass of fabric, and we still have a few days for the modiste to work her magic on both a ball gown and a wedding dress."

"I don't know how to act at a ball."

"Nonsense, my dear. You teach deportment, so of course you know how to act at a ball. You do dance, don't you?"

"Yes, but—" Thea gulped, and Will's gaze caught on her throat. Her very pale, very delicate, very fragile throat. So small and narrow that his palm would span it. "But I wouldn't want to be on display."

Lady Stone plowed straight on, apparently not listening. "And you, Mr. Archer?"

He nodded. "My mother insisted I learn, but I have had few opportunities to practice. I, too, would not care to have attention called to my lack of finesse."

"Good. It's just as well to do it this way, then. Being the guests of honor at your own ball would mean you'd have to lead the dancing, among other things. Perhaps it would focus too much attention on you."

Thea nodded firmly, as if she couldn't agree more.

"At this party, you'll be just another couple among my many guests – but you'll still meet enough people and be seen by enough of the *ton* that by the time next Season starts, you'll no longer be a matter of mystery. No one will have reason to ask questions about your bona fides."

The words were perfectly bland and absolutely factual; a casual listener would hear only a mild comment about the *ton*'s fixation on gossip. But Lady Stone's underlying tone held a warning. Will wondered if Thea had heard the message, or if he had recognized it only because he had worked with Lady Stone for months.

We don't need to tell her the truth... since it seems her butler already has.

Despite what she had said to Mr. Tomlinson, it appeared to Will that servants' gossip was quite all right with Lady Stone after all – as long as the servants only confided in *her*.

* * *

"Took long enough to get this matter sorted out," Lord Carrington grumbled. He refilled his glass and waved the decanter in Will's direction. "Need a good slug to get you through the ceremony?"

"I wouldn't turn one down," Will admitted. He opened his briefcase and laid two copies of the finished marriage contract on his lordship's desk.

Carrington eyed the pages, closely written in Will's clerk's best copperplate script. "Getting it written out so prettily must be what took you so long. Could have had this wedding last week."

Will refused to rise to the bait. "The bishop's schedule didn't help."

"In the end, he changed his appointments, though, so he could be here when I wanted him. Smart man – knows which side his bread's buttered on. Something more people should pay attention to." He cast a look at the clock. "He'll be along any minute now. The girl's taking her own sweet time, though. I sent the carriage after her hours ago."

"She'll be here." He couldn't blame Thea for not being in a hurry. She wouldn't want to wait in the bookroom with his lordship till the bishop arrived, but the idea of socializing with Lady Carrington must be even less attractive.

He supposed it was fitting that the ceremony be held here, in the very room where the entire plan had been initiated. But it was far from a joyous venue; there wasn't a ribbon or a bow, a scrap of lace, or a garland anywhere in sight. Nothing special, in fact, to show that there was to be a wedding within the hour, except for the bouquet of daisies and lilies he'd bought on a whim this morning from a street vendor near Covent Garden.

It was enough to make him wish that Lady Stone had won her argument. She had announced she would be delighted to host the nuptials so that Lady Carrington wasn't put out in the least. But his lordship had quashed the offer without a second's hesitation, pointing out that since he was the host, it was up to him to decide the locale and also the guest list – and just because mere neighbors wanted to push their noses in didn't mean they were actually invited.

After that, Will had known better than to tell his lordship that Madame thought Thea should be married from her own home – or rather, from the school – instead of in Grosvenor

Square. It had taken all of Will's considerable powers of persuasion to get her to agree to Lord Carrington's plan. She was not going to be impressed with the bookroom, but Will thought she had too much self-control to make a fuss about something it was too late to change.

He heard a commotion from across the hall and wondered who was arriving. A moment later Lady Carrington greeted the bishop in a clear voice he felt certain was deliberately pitched so it would be overheard in the bookroom. "My lord, I'm so sorry you've been dragooned into taking part in this farce."

A masculine voice – low and rich and soothing – answered. Will tried to make out the words, but the bishop was drowned out by a snort and a laugh as Lady Stone said, "*Farce*, Penelope? How can it be anything of the sort with the bishop presiding? Why, these two will be the most married couple in London, reciting their vows before such a distinguished person."

Lord Carrington growled, "I told Jenkins not to let that woman in."

Better men than you have no doubt tried. Will bit his tongue.

"I do so love weddings," Lady Stone went on, "and I'm very fond of Thea, you know. Please, Penelope, allow me to take your place as an official witness. Oh, here's our girl now."

Will stood up, reflexively straightening his cravat.

The party trooped in. Lady Stone chattered to the bishop, her hand firmly on his arm. Lady Carrington followed, clearly reluctant, and took a seat in the far corner of the room, muttering about getting this expensive foolishness over and done with. And bringing up the rear was Madame, with Thea beside her.

Thea, wearing a cleverly-fitted walking dress in a soft clear green that made the red highlights in her hair glimmer and gave even more depth to the rich brown of her eyes.

He had seen her only in drab colors, and in gowns so lacking in style that she had looked plain, despite her glorious hair and her wonderful eyes.

But now she was beautiful. And even with doubt shadowing her face and teasing into a little line between her brows, she carried herself straight and true, head high.

Give the woman a bit more confidence, and she would be nothing short of stunning. Someday, she would make an incredible countess.

Will was bemused by the very thought. He was not in the habit of looking ahead to the day when he would have to take over the Carrington heritage. He had not been exaggerating when he'd said he hadn't wanted the position; in fact, he hadn't realized how closely he stood to the title until Robert had died. In the last six months, he'd done his best not to think of the inevitable day when the responsibility would descend on him.

Yet it seemed that deep down, even as he tried to deny the facts, he had been changing. Adjusting. Getting ready.

How very odd, how all of this was affecting him. He was an outsider who because of his profession had a clear and far from flattering view of the aristocracy, with all their foibles and failings. He had expected to feel reluctance at the very idea of someday having to take a seat in the House of Lords, of donning an earl's coronet and ermine robes for the annual opening of Parliament. How perfectly silly all that pomp and ceremony was!

And yet...

He had not expected to feel so responsible for the tenants at Monkscroft, or for the fate of the house and the estate. He had not anticipated the sense of honor, the weight of obligation, the tug of duty, the determination to maintain the family's station and carry out the family's tradition... and then to pass it all down to the next generation.

But that would be a problem for another day.

Possibly it was just the business of getting married that had sent his thoughts into Bedlam territory.

He noticed that Thea's face had turned pink, and he realized he'd been staring.

Lady Stone snorted another laugh. "I thought you'd knock him to his knees with that dress," she cackled. "You're a lucky man, Mr. Archer, that she didn't hold out for a Season of her own before agreeing to wed you. She'd have her pick of the bachelors and you might be going home alone."

"You're very... very..." Awkwardly, feeling foolish and tongue-tied, he held out the flowers. "Let's get the ceremony behind us."

"After the contracts," Thea said.

Will felt his face heating. What kind of a solicitor forgot about the contracts?

Lady Carrington sniffed. "So typical of this girl, to be thinking about money at such a time. But of course that's her only thought, so I suppose the timing doesn't matter."

Will dipped a pen in Lord Carrington's inkwell and signed, then held out the pen to Thea. Her signature was a bit shaky, he noted. They stood shoulder to shoulder watching as his lordship scrawled his name on both copies.

The bishop stepped forward. "And now for the vows."

The ceremony itself was a bit of a blur. Will wondered, as he and Thea stood side by side in front of the bishop, if that was the typical state of a man making this sort of commitment, or if his skittering thoughts were unusual. How much his life had changed in a matter of days – because no matter how long it seemed, it *was* only days since the whole thing had started, right there in Lord Carrington's bookroom.

Thea stumbled over his name when she repeated her vows, and her hand was small and cold and shaky in his as he slid the marriage ring onto her finger. Or was it his own hand which trembled just a little?

The announcement that he could now kiss his bride came as a bit of a shock – and not only to him, for Thea looked up at him hesitantly. Her eyes were big, darker than usual, and full of questions. He brushed his mouth against hers and was startled at how warm her lips were, and how soft. If he'd thought about it, he'd have assumed that little about her would be soft, because she was such a determined little thing.

He barely registered that the thing was done until Lady Stone said, "No wedding breakfast, Penelope? Of course, I understand you're not feeling up to entertaining a crowd yet.

But it does seem a shame to rob these youngsters of such an important part of their special day."

Will cleared his throat. "Not at all, Lady Stone. We don't care about such things, do we, Thea?"

Lord Carrington snorted. "He's eager to get her off to himself. Get this marriage started off right. And I must say I heartily approve."

Thea turned red. Madame seemed to think his lordship was suddenly invisible, for she looked straight through him. Lady Carrington sniffed disdainfully.

Lady Stone said, "If you didn't have such an exalted title, Carrington, one would think you were crude. Well, there's plenty of time for celebrating, and we'll consider my ball tomorrow to be just the start. You all know how much I love having an excuse for a party. Now, Bishop, I need to talk to you. Won't you stop by and take luncheon with me, so we can have a comfortable coze? Unless the newlyweds would like to join us, of course."

Thea said, under her breath, "Can we just go?"

"Of course. We'll see Madame back to Bedford Square and then we'll go on to Finster's Hotel where I've taken rooms for us."

She looked horrified. "Why?"

"Because even though you demanded a home in London, it will be a few days before we can actually move in."

"But a hotel? There's no hurry about looking for a house, and I need to be at the school."

He didn't like that idea at all, but he didn't particularly want to think about why. "If you're inviting me to move in there with you—"

Her face was so red she practically glowed. "That's out of the question. There would be no space for you."

"I could always share your bedroom," he suggested, very quietly. He was so far off balance himself that it was almost comforting to see this flustered, fluttering, almost-stammering young woman. Perhaps it was mean of him to tease her – but something about his own discomfort urged him to find out just how far she could be pushed.

"Absolutely not," Thea snapped.

"It *would* shatter Madame's rule about gentlemen on the premises, if I were to live under the same roof with all your students."

"Exactly. Until we have a house, I'll remain at the school and you can stay in chambers. There's no sense in wasting money on a hotel."

He gestured toward the two copies of the marriage contract still lying on Lord Carrington's desk. "Fortunately, we now have plenty of money. And going to separate places immediately after the wedding ceremony is no way to convince his lordship that we are sincere."

"I don't care about convincing him," she muttered.

"Then how about convincing the rest of society? Shall I ask Lady Stone's opinion of a newly-married couple separating on their wedding day?"

Thea shot a look over her shoulder. "No! She'd probably offer to take us in."

And offer us one bedroom. He couldn't quite decide if he found that idea humorous, or intriguing. No – it was humorous. Definitely not intriguing. Or inviting. Or seductive.

He dragged his thoughts back to the point. "In any case, as I said, it will only be for a few days, until we can move into our new home." She stared at him, and Will went on gently, "The house I have already found for us."

Chapter Six

Thea couldn't get her breath. She'd been afraid of this kind of overbearing, dominating, *you'll-do-as-I-say* sort of husband, but then she'd talked herself out of worrying about it. She'd convinced herself that Will was kind, gentle, nice – so he would never bully her. What a fool she had been! She'd said her vows and within minutes the calm and reasonable Will Archer – the one who had listened to her opinions and soothed her fears – had turned into this... this *monster*.

She finally found her voice. "You didn't consider consulting me about something as important as where we live?"

"No – because you're obviously in no hurry to set up housekeeping. *Until we have a house* could be a very long time indeed if it was left to you to find something you approve of."

He had a point. But no man considered the same sorts of things in looking for a home that a woman did. And why was he in such a rush?

"Perhaps it will set your mind at ease to know that I have leased the place, I did not buy it. If you hate it, you have six months to find something that suits you better."

That news should have been a relief. Still, he didn't seem to realize she ought to have had a say – and that last statement had almost been a challenge.

She settled into disapproving silence. Not that her reaction seemed to disturb her new husband, who chatted easily with Madame all the way from Grosvenor Square to the school. The two of them seemed to be getting along just fine, and Madame seemed far more comfortable with Will than Thea was.

She wondered what had really happened in that hour the two of them had spent shut up together in Madame's sitting room – a discussion in which, it had been made plain to Thea, she was not welcome to participate.

Afterwards, Will had said only that Madame had asked difficult questions but seemed to accept his answers. And Madame had been very close-mouthed. At least she no longer argued whether the wedding should be delayed, though actual approval really would have been too much to hope for. And she did seem to like Will well enough.

Of course Madame didn't have to go off to a hotel with him. But then, did Thea really have to, either?

"I'm going to stay at the school," she announced as the carriage turned onto Charlotte Street and pulled up at the curb. "No one will possibly know where I am, anyway. It's not as though Lady Carrington will be coming to call."

Madame looked her over sternly. "Your place is with your husband, Thea. Your mind seems to be elsewhere just now – so I think your students will be better off without you today."

Too late, Thea realized that she'd been so lost in her own thoughts that she'd burst into their conversation – and no doubt interrupted some priceless bit of advice Will had been giving Madame.

He stepped down from the carriage and handed Madame out. Just as Thea started to follow, he shut the carriage door almost in her face. By the time Thea had pulled herself together and climbed down – awkwardly, since there was no strong arm to lean on – he had delivered Madame to the front door and returned with Alice. The maid was carrying a small valise and Will had a second, larger one.

Thea eyed him narrowly.

"I asked Alice to pack a few things for you, just enough for a few days," he said cheerfully. "And I thought you'd be more at ease at the hotel with her to take care of you."

"Such a nice holiday it will be for me, Miss... I mean ma'am. I mean Mrs. Archer. I've never stayed at a hotel, you see."

Thea wanted to say she didn't need taking care of, but she couldn't bring herself to squash the girl's excitement. "Neither have I, Alice."

"No wonder you were hesitant," Will murmured as he helped Thea back into the carriage. "New experiences are always a bit frightening."

That was true – though the new experience giving Thea pause wasn't the hotel, exactly. But Will *had* thought about her comfort, providing her with clothing and a companion. Surely he wouldn't have arranged for Alice to come along if he intended to press for his conjugal rights. Would he?

The hotel was not as big as Thea expected, and it wasn't particularly grand. But it was a bustle of movement from the moment the carriage drew up in front. The landlord himself helped to unload the valises, and the entire staff seemed impressed by the Carrington crest on the door panels, as well as confused when the carriage simply dropped them off and departed.

"Our new house has a mews," Will said. "Not enormous, but it's spacious enough for a few horses and a carriage or two."

Thea wondered irritably if he'd paid as much attention to the house itself as he obviously had to the stables.

She followed the landlord up the stairs to a room which seemed almost filled by a four-poster bed. Alice looked around, as wide-eyed as Thea felt.

"Alice can be in with you, if you don't mind," Will said, "or upstairs in the staff quarters."

Thea didn't take her gaze off the bed, which was huge and almost square, with posts stretching nearly to the ceiling and velvety hangings to close the occupants – *occupant!* – away from the world. "I want her here with me," she said firmly.

The landlord bowed. "Yes, my lady... ma'am. There's a trundle tucked away underneath the bed. Just let the chambermaid know when you want it set up."

After I'm in bed myself, Thea thought, *or I'll have to climb over it to get under the covers.*

"I'll leave you to get settled," Will said. "Since there was no wedding breakfast, I've ordered a meal to be brought up to the sitting room next door."

"And you?" Thea kept her tone carefully casual. "Will you be going to your chambers?"

"My clients, like your students, can exist for one day without me. Though I do have some paperwork that requires attention."

Relief surged over her at the idea that he didn't intend to abandon her in this new environment. Then she called herself foolish. Even if he had left, she wouldn't be alone; she had Alice. Bringing the girl *had* been thoughtful of him.

She watched as Alice unpacked the valises, only half listening to her eager chatter. When she heard dishes clattering from the next room, she went to peek in and found a serving maid lifting plates from a big serving tray. "Thank you," she said. "We can serve ourselves."

"Yes, ma'am. I'll just show your maid down to where staff takes their meals." The young woman bobbed a curtsy and swept Alice out of the room.

"Well, that was unexpected," Thea muttered, and went to investigate the contents of the tray.

"But it's pleasant to have you to myself," Will said behind her.

She jumped and looked around. How had she missed seeing him, or the table in the corner where a briefcase stood and papers were scattered over the surface?

Will picked up a plate. "May I serve you? I asked the landlord to send up a variety, since I have no idea what sorts of dishes you prefer."

Thea didn't think she could swallow food right now. The reminder that she had actually married someone who knew so little about her made her throat hurt. "Anything will do for me. One cannot be hard to please in a school environment, for it would lead the girls to do the same, and such affectations are hardly attractive."

He tipped his head to look curiously at her. "But now you will be able to order whatever you wish to eat. Have you truly not given any thought to the benefits of having your own home, as well as the responsibilities?"

"Of course I understand what is involved. I've helped in

running the school," she said defensively. "Ordering supplies, supervising staff."

"Helped – but you haven't been in charge. It's all right to be frightened of something new, Thea." He set her plate on the table, held her chair, and went back to begin serving himself. "And there are good things about being able to make your own choices."

"I'm not frightened." But she *was*, she realized. Being the mistress of an establishment was far different from helping to run one. At the school, the final decisions, the final responsibilities had all been Madame's. Now they would be hers. She would be the one who hired and fired.

Panic gnawed at her; she had no idea how to even begin. How big a house had he chosen, and how much staff would be required? Surely they wouldn't need a butler – and a good thing, too, since she had no idea where to begin looking for one. How was she to know which woman would be a good housekeeper and which might be tempted to steal by padding the account books? How did one choose menus? – She knew no more about Will's tastes in food than he knew about hers.

If he'd been looking for a way to illustrate how ill-prepared they were to be married, he couldn't have found a better one.

"It's all new for me, too, but we can learn together." With his plate filled, Will sat down at the head of the table, to her left. "That's one of the reasons I chose the house I did – because the staff will stay on."

She felt both relief and hesitation. At least she wouldn't have to start from nothing to find the necessary servants, and they should already know their jobs. But to come into an established hierarchy... would she feel like a perpetual guest, rather than the mistress of the house? "That's odd, surely, to leave all the servants behind?"

"Not in this case. The owners do not reside there but lease the house furnished and staffed. This year's tenants came to London for the Season but are now moving back to the country, or to Bath, or ... well, it hardly matters where they go, so long as they're going."

She toyed with a bit of roast chicken. "So soon? Surely the Season will continue for weeks yet. I believe Lady Stone said she would not return to the country until the end of June."

Will looked up from the thick slice of roast beef he was cutting and smiled. "I was told this family accomplished their purpose by marrying off a daughter, so they gave up the lease early. With so many people here for the Season, there are not a lot of houses available at this time of year."

That fact hadn't occurred to Thea. Perhaps he hadn't been quite as high-handed as she'd thought when he rented something so quickly and without taking time to consult her.

"As soon as the last of the family possessions are loaded and sent off, we can move in. And we can be much more comfortable there than in a hotel."

Thea cut another bite of chicken and pushed it around on her plate. "I can see that doing your work here will not be easy. Too much noise, and too many distractions."

"Indeed." His gaze rested thoughtfully on her.

Did he consider her a distraction? No doubt... but she could do something about that. "Perhaps Alice and I will walk over to the school after all. It isn't far, is it? It didn't seem so in the carriage."

"A short, brisk walk will take you to Bedford Square. But I have a better idea."

She gave up on food and looked up at him warily.

"We can go explore the house. I haven't seen much of it, because the family was still in residence. But they were to depart yesterday, so it's only their possessions which remain, waiting for the carters to take over."

She suppressed a shiver at the idea that he'd rented the place without looking at anything except – possibly – the stables. But if she were honest, the house hadn't sounded at all bad. If a family bent on marrying off a daughter during the Season had chosen to live there, then the neighborhood was acceptable and the accommodations at least adequate.

And if her options were to go look at a house or stay here, trying to be very quiet so that Will could work... what kind of a choice was that, really?

She was startled that he didn't summon a hansom when they came out of the hotel but offered his arm instead. How quickly she had grown accustomed to riding, rather than walking. She looked around, trying to get her bearings. "The house is even farther from the school?"

"Not a great deal. We can walk to it in just a few minutes."

From the hotel, perhaps, but how far was the house from Charlotte Street? She kept the complaint to herself, however. For a few minutes, in the heat of her irritation with him, she'd forgotten that she still needed Will's help.

"About the school," she began tentatively. "Could we perhaps go together and talk to Mr. Ballard? If he's dealing with a man rather than with women...especially a young woman... it might make a difference. Perhaps he'd take you more seriously."

"I have already talked to him. And before you get all bristly with me for putting my fingers into something that isn't my business, I called on him because Madame asked me to."

"And...?"

"I thought perhaps the additional roof leaks Madame told me about would induce him to be more reasonable, but he was adamant. I then talked to the prospective buyer."

"You found him?"

"In a sense, he found me."

Thea was barely listening. "And you told him about the roof and everything? What did he say?"

"That he didn't care about the condition of the building and he had taken the potential for such flaws into account when he made his offer."

Thea stared at him in dismay. "But that doesn't make any sense. How could he pay so much money and not care that the roof is full of holes?"

"He did not explain, but since he is a builder by trade I assume his plans include renovations. Or perhaps he is even farther-sighted. Since the British Museum collections are growing ever-larger, plans are being made to replace Montagu

House with a new and more suitable building – which would make the properties along Charlotte Street quite valuable."

That possibility had not occurred to Thea, for the museum had always been the quietest of neighbors. The things inside – interesting though they might be – were only available to view by appointment, so few people came and went. Why would a new building be necessary?

Will mused, "If Mr. Tomlinson owned a structure right in the middle of that planned construction, he'd be in an enviable position, able to name his price. Or he might offer to trade his property for work in building the new museum."

"You mean give it away?"

"That sort of job would doubtless put far more profit in his pocket than the school building is worth."

"That all seems a bit underhanded."

"Of course it is. But Mr. Tomlinson seems to be the sort who always has an eye to turning any situation to his advantage."

"How did you happen to discover him? And what did you mean, *he* found *you*?"

"I encountered him elsewhere and asked to consult him about repairing a roof. When he found out exactly which roof I was inquiring about, he told me not to bother because he had already arranged to purchase the building for himself."

"But Mr. Ballard promised Madame another two weeks!"

"Mr. Tomlinson seemed quite certain nothing would interfere with the bargain."

"He must come around. He must give us the chance, now that we have the money."

"That's not quite accurate."

Thea frowned. "Which part?"

"All of it. Mr. Ballard does not have to make allowances or give special consideration to a tenant. The building is his and he can sell it as he wishes. And we don't yet have a thousand guineas in hand."

"But once we sell the jewels..."

"Even that will take a little time to arrange, so I suggested they be left in the safe for the present. Here we are."

But what about the school? He had assured her they would save the school.

She wanted to shriek or perhaps burst into helpless tears; she wasn't sure which. But they were on a public street with people walking by, so for the moment she swallowed her despair.

Away from the bustle of the commercial streets, the square he had brought her to was pleasant, quiet, and somehow very green, as though spring had advanced into summer here. The park in the center was smaller and the gardens less formal than those in Grosvenor Square, but it was a more inviting prospect for a gentle stroll or a place to sit and chat. "Where are we?"

"Bloomsbury Square. It is not the most stylish part of town, but also not the least fashionable quarter."

"How far is it from the school?"

"Less than a mile, but I don't think you'll find it inconvenient."

Thea shook her head. "That will be quite a long way to walk when the weather gets cold. But I suppose if you get your stable set up... still, it will be a nuisance to have to order a carriage every day."

"You needn't do anything of the sort."

"If you're suggesting that I give up my involvement with the school—"

"I do wish you'd stop assuming that you know what I mean, Thea."

Since the school wouldn't be in Charlotte Street anymore, she would have no cause to walk there. She felt like a fool. An unhappy and angry fool.

"This is your new home," Will said.

She looked up at a tall, narrow town house, one of a row that faced southwest toward the garden in the center of the square. The facade was brick rather than stone – she could imagine what Lady Carrington would say about *that* – but the paint looked fresh and the entire structure seemed to be neatly kept. Four – no, perhaps there were five levels; the windows on the topmost floor were small and half-hidden behind ornamental iron railings.

"Very nice," she said, not meaning anything of the sort. She could hardly feel enthusiastic about a house when her entire reason for entering into this incredibly foolish marriage had just been swept out from under her.

Will raised an eyebrow and tapped the knocker on the glossy red door, and a moment later it swung open.

A very proper butler gave the smallest of bows and stepped back to invite them in. "Good afternoon, sir."

"Fenton, this is Mrs. Archer."

A little shiver ran up Thea's spine. It had been one thing when Alice used her new title, but something about hearing the words from Will's lips was different. He didn't sound possessive, exactly – but what *was* that tone in his voice? Whatever it might be, it only reminded her that it was too late to change her mind. Whether he kept his word or not, marriage was forever.

She tried not to think about it and looked around instead at the entry hall, which was nicely proportioned and pleasantly decorated. Not, perhaps, exactly to her taste, but then she had never had much occasion to think about what her taste might be. The furnishings in her bedroom at the school had been mostly left over, or retired when new beds and wardrobes were purchased for students.

That was yet another thing for her to learn – what kinds of furnishings she liked. And with the school closed, she thought bitterly, she would have plenty of time to consider.

Will handed over his hat and walking stick to the butler and laid both hands on Thea's shoulders to take her wrap. "I hope it's a convenient time for her to have the tour we discussed?"

"Of course, sir. Ma'am. As you wish. Your visitor is already here, sir."

"Visitor?" Thea asked. "We have a visitor before we've even taken up residence?"

"Then we'll look at that side first, Fenton."

"Very good, sir."

Thea gave up her wrap and Will ushered her through a

door she hadn't noticed because it was so carefully fitted into the cream-colored paneling of the wall. The hallway beyond was a mirror image of the one they'd just come from, except that the room was so empty it echoed when she spoke. "I thought you said the house was being let with the furniture."

"That's the other half. This half has been empty for months while it was being repaired and redecorated."

Thea turned in a circle, looking at the freshly-varnished staircase, the polished marble floor, the door – exactly like the one they'd knocked on, except it was dark green instead of red – and the empty fireplace nestled along one side of the room so the entry could serve as a reception room. Frowning, she turned to Will. "I don't understand."

A firm step sounded, boot heels clicking on the marble, and Madame came through a doorway under the staircase. "There you are. I'm afraid I couldn't keep myself from wandering off and looking around, Mr. Archer."

But why had he invited Madame along on an inspection tour of their new house?

Will seemed amused and not at all annoyed. "Do you think this will serve the purpose, Madame?"

Thea had never seen Madame so overcome. Her eyes were misty, her voice soft. "I couldn't ask for anything more perfect, Mr. Archer. The bedrooms are larger and there are more of them. The reception rooms will work beautifully, and the kitchen is much more convenient." She smiled. "You look confused, Thea. It's the new location Mr. Archer found for the school. Just think! With more space, we'll be able to take on a few more pupils to board, as well as more day students. Now that we don't have to buy the building from Mr. Ballard, we can afford to hire several more teachers. And the roof doesn't leak!"

"It had better not," Will agreed. He looked down at Thea. "It's a double house – half for us to live in, half for the school. And instead of walking a mile or ordering a carriage when it's time for you to teach a class, you can just come downstairs and through this connecting door."

Thea was too overcome – and too embarrassed – to speak.

Her hands fluttered to her cheeks, pressing hard. He had done all this in just a few days? While he was working out the marriage contracts with Lord Carrington and conducting all his regular business, he had not only discovered how hopeless her plans were but he had also managed to find a new and perfect location for the school instead?

And she had sniped at him for leasing a house without consulting her!

"A connecting door which I assure you, Mr. Archer, will remain locked at all times," Madame said.

"Of course – to keep gentlemen off the school premises."

"Oh, no. As our patron, *you* are welcome anytime, Mr. Archer. But I wish to protect your privacy from curious students." Madame smiled. "I know my girls very well, you see."

Thea tried to blink back tears of joy. "It's.... it's very nice." Her voice was rough and low. "I – I don't know what to say, Will. It's everything we could ask for. How did you find something so perfect?"

She hadn't realized Fenton had followed them through the connecting door until he spoke. "The owner purchased this half of the building just last year, ma'am, intending to make this a second rental to be offered on the same terms as the house next door. But the refurbishing work took longer than expected."

Will added, "Perfectly sensible, really. Once it was clear it wouldn't be ready in time for the Season, the new owner opted not to hurry the work or tie up capital in furnishings. It will be nearly a year now before *ton* families will once again be looking to rent town houses. But for the school, an empty building is far better than a furnished one. And one that's been newly reconstructed from top to bottom–"

"But you said it was a six-month lease?" Now that she had seen this perfect answer to their problem, she was terrified of losing it.

"I'm quite certain we can arrange to stay on – if you like it."

"Of course I like it!"

His dark eyes lit with a glow she'd never seen before. "You haven't even seen the other side, Thea. The house you'll actually be living in."

He was laughing at her, but she had no grounds for complaint, because he was right. After all the fuss she had made... "Very well, we'll go and look. Madame? Would you care to accompany us to inspect the rest?"

"Oh, no, my dear. I wouldn't dream of intruding. It should be just the two of you, walking through your first home and dreaming of your life together. I'm going to look around a little more, and then I must get busy organizing a move."

Thea's heart sank. "You'll need me to help."

"I will not take you away from your husband. What lovely memories you will make here – and they start now, as you explore together." She smiled, the sort of delighted glow that Thea hadn't seen from Madame in months. "And I do hope you will have fun exploring... *everything*."

They said goodbye and followed Fenton back through the connecting door. "How did you find this?" she asked Will as they trailed the butler through the ground floor. Dining room, breakfast room, library, drawing room... all adequately furnished, all quite pleasant, but nothing made much of an impression.

"I saw the signpost on the empty half, and when I came to look at it to see if it might suit us, I noticed the movers at work on the occupied side. So I inquired and Fenton told me about the circumstances."

The butler led them up the stairs. Bedrooms, sitting rooms, dressing rooms, even the luxury of a room set apart for bathing. A room done in red, one in blue, one in gold. Thea would have lost count, if she'd bothered to try to keep track. But even as staff bustled around, packing up the personal belongings which the family had been left behind, Thea could feel that the house itself was peaceful and inviting.

As they returned to the stairway, Fenton said, "The next floor is also bedrooms, along with the nursery."

"Oh," Thea said, and felt her cheeks flushing. "I don't need to see that." She declined the offer of a visit to the kitchen, refused to intrude on the servants' privacy to inspect their quarters on the topmost floor, and declared herself, as they said goodbye, to be very well satisfied.

"Though I have my doubts about that," Will said as they walked back from Bloomsbury Square to the hotel, "since you barely saw the house at all."

Thea couldn't look at him. "You mean because I didn't care to inspect the nursery?"

"No – because you were too starry-eyed to notice anything."

"I looked!"

"What color is the drawing room?"

"It's a very pleasant room. The light is quite nice, and…"

Will laughed. "It's just as well, I suppose. You'll have plenty of time to inspect the wallpaper – and in the meantime I really must get some work done. Some of my other clients have business that is just as pressing to them as Lord Carrington's."

"And Madame's." She caught her lower lip between her teeth. "You've done so much for Madame. I should have known you wouldn't dismiss my feelings. I should have known you'd manage it all. I'm so sorry, Will."

He held the door for her and kept her close to his side in the crowded hallway. The hotel was just as busy, just as noisy, as when they'd first arrived a few hours earlier. Even the sitting room reserved for them wasn't truly quiet; she could hear other guests coming and going outside, along with traffic on the street.

Suddenly she was looking forward to the peaceful, gentle murmur of the house on Bloomsbury Square. And that, she reflected, was another problem that Will had devoted himself to solving, while she had pouted and acted like a spoiled child. "I've been awful to you."

"Yes, you have, rather." His voice was matter-of-fact. He moved across the room to where his papers waited.

She should leave him to it. But it suddenly felt very important that he not think badly of her. Or at least, that he not believe she was always so difficult to please, so quick to judge. "Will, I'm not usually such a..."

"Fishwife?" he said calmly.

Thea's face felt scorched. "I suppose I deserve that. It's just that the school is so important to me."

He seemed to be sorting his papers, and he didn't look up.

"I want you to know... I *do* have a sharp tongue sometimes, but truly I'm not like... like my father."

He seemed to have focused so quickly on his work that she was surprised when he came back to stand in front of her. "Is that what's bothering you?"

She nodded, but she couldn't quite meet his eyes. "You've been all that's kind, and I've been..." Her voice was small. "It's no wonder you don't want to be married to me."

"It wasn't my first choice," he admitted. "Any more than it was yours."

There was no reason why the truth – even such a baldly-stated one – should make her feel hollow. But she did.

"And we've – *I've* – started out badly," she said. "But now that it's done and there's no way out, I promise I will make the best of it. I *can* be pleasant, and cooperative, and..." She stumbled to a halt, for he had taken her hand and was slowly drawing off her glove. The gentle brush of his hand sent warmth throughout her body – and how was that possible, anyway, when he was touching only the leather and not her skin?

When her hand was bare, he raised it to his lips, gently brushing each fingertip before letting his mouth linger against the back of her hand. Then he turned it over and pressed his lips against her palm.

Even the kiss at the end of their wedding, startling though it had been, hadn't felt as intimate as this soft exploration of her bare hand. Heat flared deep inside her.

"You're right," he said thoughtfully. "You're not like your father. I've never been the least bit tempted to do that to Lord Carrington."

"That was *not* –" She tugged her hand away from him, and regretted it as the cool room air replaced his heat. "I was trying to apologize, you – you—"

He was laughing, and suddenly her tears brimmed and threatened to overflow.

Will sobered abruptly. "Thea, stop. You've said you're sorry, very nicely indeed. I accept your apology. But that's the end of it. Don't go so far in trying to change my opinion of you that you're not fun anymore."

"I'm glad I amuse you." She tried to turn away.

He stopped her with a gentle hand on her arm. "Yes, you amuse me – but I'm not laughing at you. You have an unusual view of the world, and I like when you share it with me. Don't assume that I want you to be a milquetoast miss with no opinions of your own."

She thought about that, and then raised her face to his. "Truly? You think I'm fun?"

His eyes gleamed, not with laughter but with something else – something that felt mysterious, edgy, and just a little dangerous.

He reached out to brush a tear from her lashes, then smoothed a curl which had come loose. She held her breath as his hand slipped from her hair to cup her cheek. He bent his head, and before she could move – before she could even recognize his intention – his lips were brushing hers. Softly. So softly.

She once more felt the odd little ripple that had run over her when he kissed her at the end of the wedding ceremony. She'd thought her strange feeling was because the bishop was watching, and all the witnesses, and because she'd never been quite so close to a man before.

But there was no audience now, so that couldn't be it. There were only the two of them, in a room which seemed to have grown suddenly far too warm.

And he didn't stop kissing her. His mouth moved gently against hers, nibbling, toying, then coming back with a firmer pressure, as though he were asking a question. The tip of his tongue teased gently against her lips.

He drew her even closer than at the wedding, with one arm around her shoulders, the other hand still cupping her cheek. His body was hard and warm against hers. Her curves seemed to fit just right against the hard planes of his chest, of his thighs, of his...

She gasped at the sensation and he seized the opportunity to deepen the kiss. He tasted interesting... different... intriguing, with a hint of something wild about him, something that called to her. She wanted to press herself closer.

Instead she pulled away, staring up at him wide-eyed.

"You've never been kissed before," he said. It didn't sound like a question, and his voice was a little rough.

"Of.." Her vocal cords weren't working quite right. "Of course I have. At the... wedding."

"That doesn't count. I should have said you've never been properly kissed before."

"There was nothing *proper* about your behavior, Mr. Archer!"

He smiled. "And there she is. The feisty Thea is back, and the penitent one has been banished. Good – I was starting to worry about you. Another minute and you'd have been vowing to obey me in all things, and we can't have that."

She tried to regain her balance. "Don't you have work to do? And I..."

"Yes, Thea? What are you going to do with the rest of your day, besides think about that kiss?"

She turned her back on him. He laughed softly, and she listened as he strolled toward the table where his papers waited. What had he done to her? She seemed tuned to his every movement. How had she ever thought this room was noisy? He lit a taper from the fireplace and used it to kindle a lamp; she heard the wick hiss as the flame caught. And she could hear each breath he took, soft though the sound was.

It was unfortunate Alice hadn't thought to pack a book or two for her. But she'd think of something to keep her mind occupied... because she was *not* going to spare another thought for that kiss.

* * *

They made an oddly-assorted pair as they climbed into the hansom cab for the ride across London to Grosvenor Square, for Will was already formally dressed for Lady Stone's ball while Thea was wearing one of her ordinary walking dresses. This one was a drab gray that even managed to steal the shine from her hair. Just seeing her wear that life-draining color made Will long to pile up every dress she owned – except for the green one she'd worn for their wedding – and set them afire.

And not just because it would be fun to see her wearing nothing but her shift – though he couldn't deny the thought had crossed his mind dozens of times in the full day since he'd kissed her.

He still didn't quite know why he'd done it, except in that moment she'd been so fragile and so bent on self-humiliation that he'd have tried almost anything to stop her from flagellating herself. Kissing her had seemed a good way to jolt her back to normal. And, of course, he had been curious whether her lips really were as soft and sweet as they'd seemed when he'd tasted her so briefly at the end of the wedding ceremony.

The kiss had jolted her, all right. Only it had jolted him even more. He had expected to get his face slapped or his toes stomped on. Instead, she had melted in his arms, and that had sent his brain reeling, and before he could control himself, he'd taken things further than he'd ever planned.

He didn't regret it, because he knew now that Thea's passion for the causes and people she cared about reflected an inner fire, one that held a great deal of promise for other kinds of passion. And also, his body had learned that her soft curves would feel oh so good without all those layers of fabric between them.

When they had met, the sharp edge of her tongue had been the least attractive thing about her. But somehow in the days since, the trait had grown on him as he'd begun to see that even her more abrasive comments came about because she cared so much about something, or more often someone, that she couldn't contain herself.

"I'm still not sure we should go this evening," she said.

"Not go?" Alice sounded scandalized. "But you can't want

to miss going to a ball, Miss Thea. Think of the dancing!"

"That's partly what's bothering me."

Will shrugged. "Lady Stone would be very disappointed to learn that you would prefer spending the evening alone with your husband over attending her party."

"Don't flatter yourself. I just don't feel ready to face the *ton*." She brightened. "Perhaps the modiste won't have finished my dress after all. If I have no ball gown, I can't be expected to attend."

"If the modiste failed to keep her promise, Lady Stone would finish sewing the dress herself. Or, more likely, she'd instruct Miss Harper and Alice to do so."

"My stitches aren't nearly as neat as Madame's, Miss Thea, but I'd do my best. Oh, I so want to see the dancing."

"There, you see? You owe it to Alice to go through with this."

The hansom pulled up in Grosvenor Square, and Will helped Thea and Alice down to the pavement. "I'll see you to the door, but then I need to go and call on Lord Carrington for a moment."

Thea's brow furrowed. "Haven't you seen enough of him for a few days, at least? What is it this time?"

"Just a detail," Will assured her. "You let Alice help you get ready, and I'll be along shortly."

He waited till Lady Stone's butler had admitted them. Even from the front stoop, it was evident from the bustle of servants that the house was preparing for the start of a major social event, and he was thankful to have an excuse not to wait in the midst of the pandemonium.

He knocked on the Carringtons' door, and Jenkins admitted him. "Oh, thank heaven," the footman said. "You're here."

Will stared at him. He'd seldom heard anything more than a polite "Yes, sir" or "As you wish, sir" from this man. What calamity could have rocked the house badly enough to shake Jenkins' composure?

"They've been looking for you everywhere. His lordship sent a groom to your chambers, and even one to Miss

Winslow's... Mrs. Archer's school, to see if they knew where to find you."

"I don't understand. His lordship knew I planned to call here before Lady Stone's ball, to pick up a necklace for Mrs. Archer to wear with her ball gown."

"But that's hours away still, and he wanted you right now." Jenkins deftly relieved Will of his hat, evening cloak, and walking stick. "Best go straight in. They're in the bookroom – all of them."

"All of whom?" Jenkins must know something about what was going on. But the man's training seemed to have kicked back into operation because he merely tossed a look of silent commiseration Will's way.

Will tugged at his cravat and crossed the hall behind the footman, who tapped once on the door and opened it. "Mr. Archer, your lordship," he announced.

So the circumstances called for formality, did they?

He let his gaze sweep over the bookroom, taking everything – *everyone* – in at a glance.

Lord Carrington stood by his desk, facing off against a big, broad man who had his back to the door. On a sofa halfway across the room, Lady Carrington sat bolt upright, her arms crossed tightly over her chest. Next to her, seeming to shrink into a huddle, was a girl. No, a very young woman.

A very young, very pregnant woman.

Had Lord Carrington been up to his old tricks? No wonder her ladyship's face looked like granite.

"What are you going to do about my girl?" the big man blustered. "Her marriage papers are right there." He waved a hand at the desk. "You could at least look at them."

Marriage papers? Will couldn't believe his ears. Surely even a roué like Lord Carrington wouldn't trump up marriage papers in order to have his way with a girl.

"She's got her rights," the man went on, "and we both know it, your high-and-mighty lordship. Now what do you say about that?"

Will knew that voice. The man confronting Lord Carrington was the builder – Mr. Tomlinson.

Lady Carrington stood up. He'd been wrong about granite, for she actually smiled as she faced Will. "Mr. Archer, do come and meet Lady Calvert." Her voice sounded like melted butter. "My son Robert's wife. Soon to be the mother of his – and now of Lord Carrington's – *real* heir."

Chapter Seven

Thea had never felt so pushed, prodded, pinned and poked in her life, but she had to admit that by the time Alice, Miss Harper, Lady Stone's maid, and her ladyship had done with her, she was the most perfect version of herself that she could ever be. Her hair was curled, piled high, and sprinkled with tiny flowers and jeweled combs; her body was more tightly corseted than she had thought possible, and her neckline – or more accurately, the cleavage it displayed, pushed up and out by that impossibly-tight corset...

"I didn't realize the dress was going to be quite this – *bare*." She stared into the mirror on her ladyship's own dressing table.

"It won't be," Lady Stone said comfortably. "Alice, run downstairs and see what your master has brought. Just a little more powder, right here, I think." She touched the brush lightly to Thea's cheek.

Alice was back in minutes. "He hasn't come yet, my lady."

Lady Stone frowned. "That's not like Mr. Archer. He's had plenty of time, and I can't quite see Lord Carrington being the sort to hold him in civil conversation. Well, we'll just relax."

"Relax? I can barely breathe," Thea murmured. How on earth was she supposed to dance when she was trussed up like a Christmas goose?

"But you look so lovely," Miss Harper said. Her own dress was plainer and simpler than Thea's, but she still looked quite elegant for a companion.

"You two will be the jewels of my ball," Lady Stone announced. "Speaking of jewels..." She glanced at the clock. "What is keeping the man?"

A footman tapped at the dressing room door. "Mr. Archer, my lady."

"Finally," Lady Stone muttered. "Did it take you so long to

choose the right necklace, Mr. Archer? I knew I should have braved Lord Carrington myself."

Will closed the door and leaned against it. Thea caught a glimpse of his face – looking oddly strained – in the dressing table mirror, and turned to get a better look. "Will? What's wrong?"

He seemed to approve of the dark yellow ball gown, for his eyes widened appreciatively for a moment. Then his face tightened again. "I need to speak to you, Thea. Privately."

Lady Stone shooed Miss Harper and the maids from the room, but when Will looked straight at her and then at the door, she sniffed. "This is *my* dressing room," she pointed out. "And I'll find out what the big news is anyway, so you might as well tell me yourself. What has Lord Carrington done this time?"

"Not his lordship," Will said. His voice, normally resonant and deep and beautiful, cracked. He looked straight at Thea. "It seems as though the Carringtons' son Robert – Lord Calvert – was married shortly before his death. His widow – it seems – has presented herself to her parents-in-law." He took a deep breath. "And she's with child."

Thea's breathing grew tighter, more restricted. She couldn't even attempt to speak.

Lady Stone's eyes narrowed. "You keep saying *It seems*. Is there doubt? I'm sure Lord Carrington would not accept her word that the two were married."

"There are documents," he admitted.

"Documents can be forged."

"Not easily. Lord Carrington insists Robert had better taste than to actually marry a tradesman's brat—"

"If his lordship is anything at all," Thea muttered, "he's unoriginal. He said almost the same of me."

"No, he only said you dressed like one." A flicker of humor lit Will's eyes, but it soon died out. "Lady Carrington, on the other hand, is convinced."

"Oh, I shouldn't worry about Penelope," Lady Stone said. "If the young woman is as bad as you say—"

"Since the young woman has barely uttered a word, his

lordship isn't objecting to *her* – at least right now – as much as to her father," Will said. "Mr. Tomlinson. The builder who was working on your chimneys."

Lady Stone snorted. "That encroaching mushroom? It seems very odd, doesn't it – that he never breathed a word until now?"

"Indeed it does. He says he didn't know anything about the situation until his daughter's pregnancy became too advanced to conceal."

"How old is this girl? She could hardly be married without him knowing it."

"The papers say permission was given by the girl's aunt, which is plausible, if they were trying to keep it secret. Even if she had no legal standing – and she doesn't seem to have actually been Miss Tomlinson's guardian – that would not invalidate the marriage. If it actually took place."

"If she was married," Thea put in, "why would she have not have told her father? If not right away – or even after Robert died – surely she would have confessed when she realized she was with child."

"He says it's because he has well-known objections to aristocrats. Which seems to be true. He fawns over them in person, but he doesn't hesitate to express very definite opinions of their lack of worth when he's not face to face."

Lady Stone sniffed. "I am not surprised. But for Penelope to take up this young woman's cause does startle me. She's even more of a snob as Carrington is when it comes to social climbers. Or – of course. It sounds as if this young woman is the malleable type?"

Will nodded. "It appears so. She hardly opened her mouth."

"Penelope *would* approve of that, because she can take over and raise the child as she likes. And of course she would prefer that Robert's offspring inherit, even if the mother was not up to her standard. Far better, in her eyes, than passing the title down through Carrington's natural daughter."

Thea choked.

Lady Stone's gaze rested on her, kindly. "Oh, my dear, do think it through. Carrington's been behaving very oddly since you came on the scene. And I'm a suspicious old bird, so I made a point of noticing – which I was perfectly positioned to do, at that dinner party of mine."

Will cleared his throat. "I thought perhaps it was your butler who told you."

"He knows? I'm not surprised, but he's far too discreet to confide in me. Still, that's one of the reasons I wanted to introduce you to society myself, and right away. If I present you, the rest of the *ton* will have no reason to ask questions, and by next Season there will be another scandal taking up their attention so they'll never know they missed out on this one."

"My lady, I don't think I can..." Thea gestured at the dress. "I can't dance, and laugh, and pretend everything's all right."

"Why on earth not? Even if all this is true, there's only one chance in two that the child will be a boy – a girl can't inherit. And considering Mr. Tomlinson's fondness for neighborhood gossip, I suspect he may have seen an opportunity and seized on it."

"That has occurred to me," Will said. "He seems to be a man who always has an eye open to possibilities."

"Tomlinson," Thea said thoughtfully. "He's the one who's bought the school?"

"Yes – and the coincidences piling up make me wonder. He takes on a repair job here in the square, and is rebuffed by his lordship when he offers to work on his roof. Then I ask him about making repairs on the school, and he's unimpressed with me as well. Or am I seeing only what I want to see?"

"Because you don't want to be unseated? It sounds as though you have good reason for suspicion," Lady Stone mused. "He obviously knew you were the heir, that day we met him in the square. And he as much as admitted he'd been asking questions. An uppity lord, a dead son, a distant cousin inheriting... It must have seemed a golden opportunity."

"Proving it may be the difficulty," Will said. "I've only

glanced at the documents as yet, but there's nothing obviously wrong with them. I have to agree with Thea, though, my lady. We cannot stay for the ball. Lord Carrington wishes to call on us as soon as possible."

Lady Stone's eyebrows climbed. "The old dear must be upset, if he's putting himself out to that extent. Perhaps he's going to demand you give all the goodies back."

"I think it's more likely he wants to escape from Lady Carrington's somewhat-oppressive glee."

Thea stood up, feeling a bit unsteady. "I suppose that leaves no doubt that she knows for certain about me. Not that it matters, I suppose, but it's just as well we don't put ourselves forward right now." Was she so breathless because of the corset, or because of Will's news? "And we'd better go quickly, before your guests begin to arrive."

Lady Stone nodded thoughtfully. "Don't fret, my dears. This will work out. I'll send for the carriage to take you home."

She left the room, and Thea began to mindlessly gather up her belongings. "I think... no, I'm fairly certain I'm not really upset."

Will looked puzzled. "Truly? You don't mind?"

"I'm surprised, yes. Shocked? Definitely. But upset? No. Well, other than having to give everything back, I suppose. Do you think he'll let us keep enough to save the school?"

"That's your biggest concern? But of course it is. You never wanted anything else from this marriage."

Oh. Marriage. How had she forgotten that she'd committed herself, for life, to this man?

I only wanted to save the school. I didn't want to be married.

But even though there was no longer a reason for their alliance, now that the vows were behind them, they were bound. For life. Forever.

Yes, she was *definitely* upset about that.

* * *

Thea would have given anything to get out of the ball gown and loosen her corset, but any delay at leaving Grosvenor

Square would bring them face to face with the very Society crowd she had never wanted to meet in the first place. She didn't want to encounter Lady Stone's important friends while she was sneaking away from the ball which was to have presented her to those very people.

So she and Will were both still wearing their formal clothes – and Alice was still pouting, annoyed by getting no answers when she asked why they hadn't stayed for the dancing – when they were set down once more outside the hotel.

"I'll change as quickly as I can," Thea promised as they reached the sitting room. "When do you think – Oh. Your lordship." She made her curtsy.

"That's a definite improvement over your usual garb," Lord Carrington grunted. "Lucinda Stone has more taste than I thought she did, if she chose that dress."

I chose it, Thea wanted to say. *Except for the neckline.* But there was no point in pulling caps with him. It didn't matter anymore what Lord Carrington thought.

His lordship gestured with his brandy glass. "You couldn't have picked a hotel that offers some actual comforts, I suppose? A decent brandy would go a long way to making this place bearable." He looked around the sitting room with distaste.

"The location is convenient," Will said. "I'm surprised you're here already, sir. You didn't... ah... surely you didn't leave Mr. Tomlinson and his daughter with Lady Carrington?"

"No. They left before I could throw the bounder out and tell him to take his lying lass home and give her a good whipping. But he'll be back, I'm sure."

Thea shuddered. "Just because her father seems to be unpleasant doesn't make this the girl's fault."

Lord Carrington blistered her with a look. "Of course it's her fault. Tell me what you know, Archer. Everything you couldn't say in front of that blackguard. You've met him before?"

After Will had described the encounters he'd had with Mr. Tomlinson, Lord Carrington snorted. "So I'm right and he's making it all up."

"There are a number of possibilities."

"There you go again, you nodcock. This time you're arguing against your own interests."

"It is my job, sir," Will said levelly. "Being willing to look at all perspectives is far more conducive to reaching the truth than is taking a side and standing adamantly on it."

As you are in the habit of doing. He might as well have said it, Thea thought, because from the way his lordship's face darkened, he knew exactly what Will had meant.

"As I was saying," Will said firmly. "The story could be true. In that case, Robert married this girl with the connivance of her aunt, and they kept the fact from her father because of Mr. Tomlinson's prejudice against the nobility. Then after Robert's death she didn't know what to do, so she continued to keep silent until her pregnancy made it impossible to hide any longer. That's the first possibility."

"Humph," his lordship said.

"Secondly, the child could be Robert's, but the marriage papers are faked." Will's voice was steady.

Thea watched Lord Carrington closely. That would be the very scenario he'd tried to act on before. If Thea had been male, he'd have attempted to find a way to make the birth appear legitimate. So why hadn't he seized on this chance to put his son's child in line for the title, ahead of Will?

He didn't comment, and Will went on. "The third possibility is that the entire thing could be an attempt to establish a claim through an impostor. The young woman is with child by some other man, and Mr. Tomlinson simply seized on circumstances to insert her and her child into a wealthy, titled family."

His lordship looked more thoughtful than Thea had ever seen him. "What happens next?"

"I believe it would be wise to bring your regular team of solicitors into the picture, and let them investigate."

"Why?"

"Because they have the ability to inspect and pass judgment on the papers, to check the facts in the parish where the marriage supposedly took place, to ask official questions of Mr. Tomlinson and his daughter. It will be a sizable task."

"No, I mean why aren't you going to look into it?"

"Because I have a conflict of interest."

"Exactly. You've got the most to lose. Why aren't you eager to check it all out?"

"I will advise and consult. But if everyone is to be certain the result is accurate, it's better if I'm not too closely involved."

"I want you to take care of it."

Will stared at his lordship, eyebrows raised. "And by *take care of it*, you mean – what?"

Lord Carrington shifted his boots on the carpet, staring at his toes. "Find out the truth," he said finally. His voice was gruff. "Whatever it is."

"I would not accept the charge on any other basis, sir."

"Yes, yes. You don't need to remind me you're the self-righteous type."

"I am honored, sir." Will sounded nothing of the kind – and Thea had to admit the comment had not sounded like a compliment to her, either.

"Not that I believe a word this Cit says," his lordship grumbled.

"You are convinced Robert would never have married this girl?"

"Absolutely. Or carried on with her, either."

Is he deluded? Before she could stop herself, Thea asked, "How can you possibly be so certain?" Was it simply because Lady Carrington had been easily convinced, and he couldn't stand for her to be right? It was the best explanation Thea could think of – but perhaps it was colored by her own dislike of the woman.

"Don't look at me like that, girl. You're thinking *Like father, like son*. But you're wrong. That was an entirely different thing. You've got good blood from both sides. Your mother may have been a governess but she was a lady."

Thea drew a breath to retort – but since she had no idea

what answer she could possibly make, she let it out quietly instead.

"And I didn't throw her out. I... I didn't want her to go. But she said it was better if... She said..." Lord Carrington's voice cracked. He cleared his throat, brushed off his hat, and stood up. "When are you moving from this abominable hotel into a house?"

"Tomorrow," Will said.

"Where? I'll no doubt need to send for you again."

"Bloomsbury Square."

His lordship looked sour. "Why there? I know I told you I wouldn't pay for the most expensive place in the city, but why must you choose *that* neighborhood?" He didn't wait for an answer.

Thea listened to his steps fade down the passageway. "Well, that was unexpected." She didn't know if was from the shock or her tight laces, but her vision had gone a little orange around the edges.

"Do you believe him?"

"I don't know." She sat down abruptly. "For the longest time, I had no idea he even existed, because I thought my father had died. Then, when I found my mother's papers... it wasn't as if she left me a letter explaining it all. I had to fit the pieces together – and maybe I did it all wrong. But what was I supposed to think? A governess, and her employer?" She shook her head. "Now I don't know what to think. But that will have to wait. You said there were three possibilities, but surely they can't all be equally likely. And you must have seen this sort of thing before. What do you believe, Will?"

For a moment she thought he wasn't going to answer. His eyes were soft, worried – but he seemed to understand that she needed time, that she wasn't even close to being ready to talk about her parents. "I don't believe it was a coincidence that Mr. Tomlinson was working on Lady Stone's chimneys. But whether he sought the job with the goal of studying his lordship before approaching him with a valid claim, or if he thought up the scheme because of the gossip he heard in the square while he was working there... that I don't know."

"Why would he have investigated Lord Carrington before approaching him? If the story is true, what else could he do but bring his daughter to the Carringtons?"

"Wouldn't you want to know what sort of a family it was before you committed yourself? Before you put your daughter into the midst of these people, and into their power?"

She considered. "That actually makes me more doubtful of the claim, not less, because you're right. Once he knew more about the Carringtons, why wouldn't he have taken her straight home and protected her from them? Unless he really doesn't care about her at all."

Will smiled wryly. "One would think you're no fonder of the so-charming Carringtons than Tomlinson is. Of course, the way he ignored his daughter the entire time he was arguing with his lordship made me wonder if he sees her only as a tool."

Much the same way that Lord Carrington regarded Thea, she supposed. No matter what he might have felt for her mother, he seemed to see his daughter as nothing more than a useful chip when it came to bargaining. The thought left her feeling hollow.

Will glanced at the mantel clock. "Have you told Alice to start packing your things? I want to see you settled into the house before I begin looking into Mr. Tomlinson tomorrow. Is there anything more at the school that you will need right away, or can the rest of your possessions wait until Madame moves everything?"

"All the furniture in my bedroom there belongs to the school, and everything I actually own will fit into a single trunk. But Will – should we really move into the house? With this uncertainty..."

"There's no uncertainty about a six-month lease. And it's already paid."

"Oh. Well, that's good. At least the school will be protected for that long."

Will surveyed her thoughtfully. "Lady Stone was right, you know. Even if this is all true and Miss Tomlinson really is Lady Calvert, the child might be a girl."

Thea sighed. "So we have to live with this uncertainty for months yet."

"Don't assume the worst. We could know as soon as someone goes to Hampshire, talks to the girl's aunt, and checks the parish register."

"Hampshire? Don't the Tomlinsons live in London? If his business is here –"

"The aunt lives in Hampshire. Not far from that other country estate Lord Carrington offered us – the one that's near Monkscroft. Apparently Robert spent considerable time there, so he might have met the girl then."

"Another coincidence?" she asked quietly.

He sighed. "Perhaps."

"Will, I don't understand why he wouldn't have told his father he was married – if he was, I mean. Maybe not right away – heaven knows that wouldn't have been a pleasant conversation. But when he knew he was dying, wouldn't he have said something? Surely he would have wanted his wife to be taken care of."

Will shook his head. "Robert died in an accident. He was on a stallion no one should have been riding, he was alone, and he was thrown. It happened on that estate – the one near Monkscroft. The horse returned to the stables, the grooms searched – but he was gone by the time they found him."

"So there was no time to speak, and no one to tell." Sadness fluttered through her.

"It's late, Thea, and there's nothing more to be done tonight."

He sounded tired, distant. She wondered if it was the sudden doubt about his position, or the weight of the task ahead of him, or the tragic way Robert's life had ended, or the odd half-comments Lord Carrington had made about Thea's mother. There were certainly plenty of reasons for Will to feel out of sorts.

While she was pleased that he'd been talking to her as an equal, she was uneasily aware that his attitude had changed. Of course the situation *was* serious – but she'd come to expect that Will could find humor in almost any circumstance, and it bothered her to see him like this.

"What do you really want, Will?"

"The truth, of course."

"I wasn't suggesting you would blur the facts. But would you be so very disappointed to find this baby is the heir, and not you?"

He hesitated. His gaze flicked across her, and she saw something in his eyes that might be pain. "I think so, yes."

"I can understand that. Even though you didn't ever expect to inherit, you've always been an Archer. The family heritage has been part of you."

"I've had to get accustomed to the idea. But since it became my responsibility, I've started to look at all this as a sort of calling – taking care of the estate and maintaining the family's legacy. If that changes, of course I'll feel regret." His gaze hardened, and for just an instant she saw past the easygoing solicitor and glimpsed the aristocrat he might someday be. "While you seem to be relieved at the prospect. At least you said the idea of losing it all didn't upset you."

"Is that what's bothering you? When I said I wasn't upset, I really didn't mean that I don't care about any of this. I was just relieved not to have to face society tonight."

"No. That wasn't what you said. You were worried about the money – and only the money. Having enough to save the school."

She thought back and concluded that he was correct. That *was* what she'd said. "But you must see the whole idea of belonging to the aristocracy – the entire notion of family legacy, for that matter – doesn't matter to me in the same way it does to you. It can't, because I grew up with no idea I was anything other than a vicar's granddaughter. Good night, Will."

As she left the room, she saw him rub a hand across the back of his neck as though it hurt. But she couldn't exactly regret what she'd said, for it was the truth. They were different, in upbringing and in outlook. And they would always be different.

They'd been married just a bit more than a day, and already the rifts between them were growing apparent.

Was he, too, wishing that Mr. Tomlinson had made his move before they'd actually committed themselves with wedding vows?

For she *was* wishing that. Wasn't she?

* * *

The house on Bloomsbury Square was peaceful and quiet and calm, and it should have been welcoming. But when the housekeeper respectfully requested a few minutes of her time, and then started their conversation by rattling off a list of questions about Thea's preferences in menus, staff management, and household policies, she found herself feeling ignorant and entirely unnecessary. She felt inadequate when she had to admit that she didn't actually have a lady's maid, only Alice – and then only as a loan from Madame.

And when the questions moved on to Will's preferences, such as whether special accommodations would be required for his valet, she was lost. *Does Will even have a valet?* She supposed he must have some sort of manservant; she'd just never given any thought to how he had actually lived in chambers.

"I don't know, Mrs. Fenton," she admitted finally. "We're newly married, and–"

The housekeeper smiled. "But of course. I beg your pardon, ma'am. We'll just learn as we go along. I do hope Mr. Archer isn't the sort to lose his temper if we get it wrong at first?"

Thea shivered. *At least I'm fortunate in that way.* "No, he's not the sort to lose his temper at all."

"I hope you'll forgive me the liberty of speaking out, ma'am? You see, this is a lucky house. Every year since Fenton and I have been here, our young ladies have found love and romance, and we're all very proud of our record in getting them well-married. But you and Mr. Archer are a bit different."

Thea froze. Was it so obvious, even to the servants, that their marriage had nothing to do with love and romance?

"We seldom get to see anything of them after that, you see. The young ladies move into the homes their husbands provide, and their families go back to the country. It will be sheer pleasure to see young people who aren't seeking love but have already found it."

"Oh. Yes. Sheer pleasure." Feeling completely out of her depth, Thea firmly turned the conversation back to menus.

With that interview concluded – and she could be forgiven, she thought, for wondering who had been doing the interviewing! – she was completely at a loss for something to do. Clearly the house would run just the same, whether she was paying attention or not.

Finally she wandered upstairs and found Alice folding clothes away in the wardrobe of the largest bedroom, which looked out over the garden at the back of the house.

"When you're finished with that, I want to walk over to the school," Thea said. "I'm certain Madame will need help to plan the move."

Alice nodded silently. She still seemed to be feeling the loss of her elegant evening out. Or perhaps she, too, felt inadequate in such sophisticated surroundings.

As they turned onto Charlotte Street, Thea was startled to see carters with drays and wagons lined up in front of the school. Inside, men were stomping down the stairs under the weight of bedsteads and wardrobes and trunks.

Madame herself was in her sitting room, supervising as yet another worker took her books off the shelves and crated them.

"How did you manage to arrange a move so quickly?" Thea asked.

"Everything seemed to fall into place, once I mentioned Mr. Archer's name – and the fact that he's Lord Carrington's heir."

Thea sighed. "Well – about that..." She reconsidered. This muddle wasn't exactly a secret – or at least it wasn't likely to be for long, if Mr. Tomlinson had his way – and of course she could trust Madame. Still, discretion seemed the wiser course.

Will had gone off this morning as soon as he'd escorted her and Alice to the house, to seek out Mr. Tomlinson and make a closer inspection of the documents. It was possible that by now he'd found that the papers weren't as represented. If that was the case, the fewer people who ever knew of the claim, and the potential upheaval it represented, the better.

Thea wasn't certain that was the outcome she preferred, but at least they would know, rather than having to endure months of uncertainty waiting for Miss Tomlinson's baby to be born.

"How can I help?" she asked.

"Stay out of the way." Madame's smile took the sting out of the words. "The men are doing everything. When they have all the goods loaded, I will go over to the school and instruct them as to where to put it all. I've called the new teachers in to help next week, and the students can help get their own things put in place – at least, those who aren't going home for a bit of a holiday while we get settled in the new quarters. So there's really nothing for you to do and no reason for you to be away from your husband."

Run out and play and don't bother me. Thea knew that wasn't what Madame meant, but the dismissal bothered her anyway. Was Madame trying to ease her out?

Thea knew she was nowhere near as necessary to the operation of the school as her mother had been. Anna Winslow had been a brilliant teacher, ideally suited for a small school where everyone needed to fill multiple roles. And Anna's education – started with her father the vicar, followed by an excellent school, and continued through her life with her own reading and study – had been first-rate. If there was a single person who truly illustrated the concept of a bluestocking, it would have been Anna Winslow.

Thea had followed her mother's example. Not only was she a good student, but she had always known her role would be to fit herself into the school, and she had done her best to prepare. Given another few years, she could have done a creditable job of stepping into her mother's shoes. But at twenty-two, she couldn't fill the enormous hole Anna had left. No one could. She could only try her best and do whatever she was able in other ways – even if those actions came at considerable cost to her.

Of course Madame didn't see her action as a sacrifice. And that was exactly what Thea wanted – for Madame to believe that this was a love match, not to see Thea as a martyr. So she could hardly throw a tantrum now and demand to be praised.

The worker put the last books in the crate, nailed on the top, and with a nod, carried it out of the room.

Madame sank into her favorite chair by the fire and waved Thea to the one across from her. "I've been meaning to talk to you anyway, my dear. Your responsibilities will be changing, especially now that you have a home to establish for your husband. You may not have realized yet how much of your time that will take, but you'll have much less freedom for the school. I'll be so grateful if you can continue with the etiquette and deportment classes, but I can't ask for more of a commitment than that."

Thea said levelly, "Did Will tell you he didn't want me involved in the school?"

Madame looked shocked. "Of course not. If he was opposed, why would he have gone to all the trouble to find a new location?"

Because that was part of our deal. The new building was an outgrowth of his promise that if she married him, they would save the school. But he hadn't exactly promised anything more than that. What if he *didn't* want her to be involved day to day?

"Thea, I've devoted my life to this enterprise, and your mother did the same – even having you didn't stop her, especially after you were old enough to take part in the classes she taught. But your situation now is far different than mine, or your mother's. You have a husband to look after, and you will have a social position. Mr. Archer will expect you to entertain his clients if he continues to practice law. Or what if he goes into politics, and takes a seat in the House? He will need a political hostess. Whatever path he takes, you will need to learn your role so you're ready when you become his countess."

What if I don't want to do any of that?

"And of course someday there will be children. Mr. Archer assured me that he will not press you for a family, but—"

Thea was horrified. "You and Will talked about – about *that*?"

"Of course we did, my dear," Madame said gently. "I was acting in the light of a mother, after all. I am certain Lord Carrington did not ask those questions of your husband, so someone had to. I advised that you take time to truly get to know each other before starting a family, since you did not have the patience to do so before the wedding."

That much was true – their discussion last night had illustrated how little they had understood.

"I should have asked you this before the wedding." Madame looked uncomfortable. "Did your mother ever talk to you about... about marital relations?"

I cannot believe we are having this conversation. "You don't need to concern yourself about it," Thea said. "Of course I understand the basics." She had tried to avoid the subject when Anna had brought it up. Since she didn't ever expect to marry, she had told her mother she had no interest in the information. But Anna had insisted that any teacher of young ladies needed to know the facts. Thea could feel herself blushing even now, both at the memory of that very awkward discussion and the prospect of another one now – and suddenly she was eager to get away.

She left Alice helping to pack up the linen room and started to walk slowly back to Bloomsbury Square, trying to enjoy the sunshine and the rare feeling of being completely alone. But she had gone only a short distance before the maid came panting up beside her.

Thea's mood lifted. "What is it, Alice? Does Madame need me to return?"

Alice shook her head. "She sent me after you because a lady doesn't walk along the streets alone." Her tone was disapproving.

Thea could hardly argue, for she was the one who lectured the girls about never going out of the school building without a companion or two. But being on the receiving end of that scolding was an entirely different thing. No wonder her students sometimes rolled their eyes and sighed when she made them recite the rules.

In Bloomsbury Square, the footman admitted them and said, "Ma'am, Mr. Archer wanted to speak to you the minute you came in. He is in the library, I believe."

He must have news. Thea looked around, at a loss for a moment. "And that's – in which direction?" Will had been right; she really hadn't paid enough attention on their tour, if she couldn't find her way to the principal rooms.

She sent Alice upstairs with her spencer and bonnet and followed the footman's gesture to a door under the stairs.

Calling the room a library was a bit of a misnomer; there was a wall of bookshelves, true enough, but the books themselves looked like a ragtag collection, the kind of random volumes left behind by the families that had rented the house, rather than a careful selection. If Will was going to use this as an office, even for a few months, perhaps she could make it more inviting. Some brighter colors, softer furniture, a bigger desk.

He was sorting papers, with his briefcase open, but he looked up soberly when she came in.

It's not good news, then. "You wanted to see me?"

"I've sent for a post-chaise, and I'm off for Hampshire as soon as it arrives."

"When will you be back?"

"Not until I've discovered the truth."

That wasn't a real answer, but she supposed it was at least an honest response. "I see."

Will paused. "You did know I would likely have to go."

"Yes, but..." She tried to laugh. "At least you're not abandoning me at a hotel."

"You feel abandoned?" He turned back to his papers.

Yes. "That's not what I meant, exactly. Obviously you don't have a choice about going. I just don't feel comfortable in the house yet, and to be here alone... I suppose I can go and stay at the school after all." Except that by tonight, the school would no longer be on Charlotte Street; all the pieces would be next door and still no doubt in an uproar. It would hardly be the peaceful refuge it had once been.

He put a folded stack of pages, tied together with a flat string, into the briefcase. "Come with me."

Thea stared at him. "You don't mean it."

"Why not? The route I've planned takes us past Tanner's Close."

"What's that?"

His eyes sparkled. "The country house you demanded his lordship give you. Wouldn't you like to at least see it?"

It might be the only opportunity she'd have. Would it be better to know first-hand what she might be losing, or never to see it at all?

Will rang the bell, and when the footman answered, told him, "Instruct Mrs. Archer's maid to pack enough for her mistress for a few days in the country."

The servant nodded and withdrew.

"I didn't actually say I was going with you, Will. Do you really want me to come?" Her body felt full of bubbles, as though everything was suddenly lighter.

"You might be helpful in talking to the aunt."

The bubbles died. Still, given the choice between staying here, fretting helplessly, or seeing some of the countryside... "Then I guess I'm coming along. What about Alice?"

"Can you cope without her? The fewer people who know why we're making this trip, the better."

"She won't like being left behind."

"It might be as well, though, since soon enough you will need a lady's maid and she's not trained to the work."

He wasn't wrong, of course. Alice's ministrations were all very well for a teacher who had a simple wardrobe and limited social interaction, but she'd been little help in getting Thea ready for Lady Stone's ball; the girl had simply been overwhelmed.

Thea sighed at the idea of a real lady's maid poking and prodding at her like that every day – but Will was right. At least she could postpone the decision for a few more days. Maybe even weeks. "How long will it take to go all the way to Hampshire?"

"We'll try for Tanner's Close tonight, and sometime tomorrow we should be in the village where the aunt lives."

"So quickly?"

"The sooner we get there, the sooner our business can be conducted. It's not a sight-seeing tour. And I'm afraid a couple of days in a carriage won't feel quick at all."

The footman tapped once on the door and came in. "The post-chaise is in the street, sir."

"Thank you, Milsom." Will closed his briefcase. "And the luggage?"

"Already strapped in place, sir."

Alice was waiting by the front door with Thea's cloak and bonnet, and as Thea was settling herself into the chaise, Mrs. Fenton bustled out with a basket. "You can't go missing meals," she said firmly, "so Cook has packed a picnic for you."

Perhaps that explained her odd hollow feeling. It might not be anticipation or excitement after all – only hunger.

As soon as Will had taken his seat, the chaise drew away from the house and the post-boys threaded their way carefully through the traffic. As it swung onto the avenue which would take them onto the turnpike, the vehicle picked up speed. Thea gazed eagerly from the window at the passing scene.

"Have you ever been outside London?" Will asked.

"My mother and I went to Norfolk once, on the mail coach. I was very young."

"Why?"

"Why Norfolk? Or why the mail coach? Perhaps it was to do with the school."

"You never visited your mother's family?"

Thea shook her head. "She seldom spoke of them, and even then she would talk of nothing beyond her early childhood memories. Now I understand why she had lost contact. They must have considered her a disgrace."

"Then it was their loss," Will said quietly. "But perhaps her father was better at being a vicar than he was at being a Christian."

"I miss her so." Thea blinked away tears and tried to smile.

"You said she was a partner in the school. Was that just an expression, or did she actually own part of the business?"

"Of course Madame was the founder, so she was headmistress. But they always consulted on decisions, and always said they were equals. Why?"

"Where did she get the money to invest in a share?"

Thea nibbled at her thumbnail. "It never occurred to me to wonder. You think Lord Carrington might have... paid her off?"

"Or made certain she had a way to provide for herself. If he really did care for her..." His voice was dry. "Maybe he's actually human after all."

"I'll have to think about that." She looked out the window again. They'd passed out of the most congested areas of the city, and she could already see that the landscape might not be as fascinating as she'd hoped. "I should have brought a book to keep me company myself while you work."

"It's difficult to read, and impossible to write, at turnpike speeds. But we can while away the hours by talking."

"You brought me along to entertain you? Not just to talk to the aunt?"

"Perhaps a bit of both." He smiled. "You must admit, you can be very amusing."

He had wanted her to come after all.

Thea's bubbles came back. The odd feeling hadn't been hunger after all, it seemed, but it wasn't just anticipation or excitement either. Perhaps, she thought, this was simple happiness.

Chapter Eight

Thea had not anticipated what turnpike speed was, or how much a carriage could sway and bounce, or how very long it could take to travel across the length of a county. The sun was low in the sky by the time they reached Tanner's Close. The picnic basket had long since been ravaged, and the jolting of the carriage had left Thea fighting a headache and wanting nothing more than to climb into a bed and rest for days.

But she revived as the chaise slowed. They were not at a manor house, however, but in a charming village nestled into a little valley, in front of a small inn, and Thea sank back into the cushions. "I don't mean to whine, Will, but I thought you said that last change of horses would be the final one tonight."

"No doubt the post boys are asking directions and making arrangements for their stay and the care of the horses." And indeed, only a few minutes later they were once more on their way.

Tanner's Close was not far from the village, and as the carriage drew to a halt on the graveled drive and Thea got her first glimpse, she sat up with a start. The long rays of the sinking sun washed across the mellow brown brick facade of an exquisitely-proportioned Georgian house. Three stories tall, it boasted mullioned windows, a balustraded roof line, and four tall columns flanking the front door. There were no lights to be seen, but that was to be expected; at this hour the servants would not be in the public areas of the house.

Will leaped down from the carriage and carefully handed Thea out. "Fresh air and a good stretch will make you feel better."

One of the post boys had gone to bang on the front door, since no one appeared to have heard their approach, and Thea took a few careful steps, working out the stiffness from a long day's ride.

Finally, when she had just about given up hope, the front door opened and a footman looked out at the carriage, eyed the post boys, and said, "What do you want?"

Since there had been no time to send word ahead to warn of their visit, it was a reasonable enough question when faced with an unexpected hired carriage full of strangers. But there was something about the footman's tone that hit Thea just wrong.

"This is Tanner's Close?" Will said.

Obviously recognizing Will's voice as that of a gentleman, the footman pulled himself up straighter. "That it is. Who's asking?"

Thea waited for Will to announce that they were the new owners of the estate, but instead he said, "We are representatives of Lord Carrington, traveling across the county, and we need lodging for the night."

"There's an inn in the village," the footman said, and started to close the door.

"Lord Carrington would not be pleased to find that his house is not ready for guests. We are not going away, so please summon the butler and the housekeeper."

While the footman goggled at Will, Thea stepped over the threshold.

Will paused to speak in a low tone to the post-boy and then followed. The footman trotted away down a hall toward a half-hidden door that must lead to the service areas of the house. Thea heard the chaise's wheels crunch on the gravel as it pulled away, and Will closed the door.

"Why did you say we're only guests?" she asked.

"The notice of a change of ownership won't have reached here yet, since it was only made official two days ago. Announcing that the estate now belongs to us would, I think, be greeted with disbelief – and I don't feel like spending the entire evening arguing the point. We'll only be here for one night."

"That looks as if it may be unpleasant enough." The hall was dim, lit only by the lowering sun, but the sharply-angled rays showed dust motes floating in the air. Thea considered rubbing a fingertip along the marble top of the nearest table, but thought better of the idea because she didn't know if Alice had packed enough gloves for her to go deliberately soiling them. Instead, she took a handkerchief from her reticule and quietly rubbed it along the surface, and was not surprised to find a considerable smudge on the white linen. "Perhaps you shouldn't have been so hasty at sending the chaise on to the inn."

"I suspect we'll gain useful information by posing as random guests. Much more than if the staff knew we hold the power to turn them out of the house."

Before Thea could answer, the housekeeper bustled in. "I understand you're saying that you're Lord Carrington's guests." Doubt dripped from her voice. "He's not here, so how can you be his guests?"

"He is in London," Will said patiently. "But he arranged for us to come."

Thea had to admire the absolutely accurate but misleading statement.

"Not with me, he didn't," the housekeeper sniffed.

Will smiled at her – but it wasn't a friendly smile. "Perhaps you will have heard that his lordship's heir, after the death of Lord Calvert, is a cousin by the name of Archer? I am he."

"And I'm to believe that? Who's this, then?"

"My wife. Mrs. Archer."

Thea tried to ignore the little ripple that always ran over her at the sound of her new name in Will's deep voice.

The housekeeper was clearly not impressed – or convinced. "Now that I do know," she said firmly. "The new heir isn't a married man."

Thea sighed and decided it was past time for her to take a hand. "No wonder Lord Carrington spends no time here – though I'm surprised he has allowed the house to become a shambles."

The housekeeper bristled. "How dare you!"

"I dare because the thing is apparent. Either you don't understand your job, or you don't care. You are not prepared to receive guests, or you wouldn't keep us standing by the front door while you try to put us off. The furniture is dirty." Thea displayed her smudged handkerchief. "The footman was rude and you are impudent. You have a choice to make. Will you set the household in motion so that we have clean sheets and a fire tonight? Or shall I send a footman into the village to call our chaise back to take us to the inn, and spend the rest of my evening writing a letter to Lord Carrington advising that he turn off every servant employed on this estate, starting with you, and begin afresh? You have exactly five seconds to make up your mind."

The housekeeper's jaw had gone slack. For a moment, things hung in the balance, then she snapped her mouth shut and called, "Miller!"

The footman had been lurking nearby, listening, for he appeared within moments. "Yes, Mrs. Wells?"

The housekeeper shot a glare at Thea, but she began issuing orders as she moved off. "Fire" and "sheets" were among the words Thea caught, along with a couple of names that might have been maids.

Will was staring at her.

"What? Apparently we're staying." Thea raised her voice. "Mrs. Wells? I expect you will prepare the best bedchambers. And a light supper would not come amiss."

The housekeeper's step hitched a little. She didn't look back, but she nodded. "Yes, ma'am."

"Well done," Will said. A smile tugged at his mouth.

"Persuasion would have taken all night, so I thought it was worth imitating Madame's stern schoolmistress voice." She turned toward the door where the footman had disappeared. "I'm tired, I'm hungry, and I want to sit down. I wonder if there's a decent chair to be found."

"You didn't sound like you were imitating anyone," Will said. "You sounded like a countess."

Thea paused, startled to realize how very differently she'd reacted than she had at the London house earlier today. Had it really only been this morning that her conversation with another housekeeper had left her feeling inadequate and out of place? What had changed?

Only the situation, she decided. Mrs. Fenton obviously knew her business, and her sheer competence had left Thea uneasy about her own place in the household. But at Tanner's Close, someone needed to take charge, so she had done what was necessary. That was all.

But it would be ironic if she was learning to be comfortable in her new role, just as it threatened to slip away.

* * *

The night at Tanner's Close left a great deal to be desired, even considering that Will's standards of comfort were probably a world away from his lordship's. The chimney in his bedroom smoked till the room was gray, the hangings were so dusty he couldn't stop sneezing, and the light supper that Thea had requested turned out to be little more than bread and cheese. He couldn't imagine Lord Carrington putting up with any such discomfort, so obviously Thea had been right that the Carringtons hadn't been in residence in a long time. No wonder he'd been so amenable to passing the estate along to Will and Thea.

But it wasn't the lumpy mattress or the sketchily-aired sheets or even his lordship's sharp dealing which kept Will awake. It was the sudden appearance of yet another side of Thea – as sharp-tongued as she'd ever been, but with an added edge. She hadn't been cruel, or demeaning, or unfair; she'd simply demanded proper treatment, and the housekeeper had responded almost in spite of herself.

He'd done his new wife a disservice, thinking she resembled the man who had sired her. She was nothing like the vain and self-centered Lord Carrington.

Will had found her incisive handling of the housekeeper to be oddly arousing. Which was completely ridiculous, of course.

He finally drifted off to sleep thinking of Thea in the room next to his, wondering if she slept curled up or stretched out.

In the morning, their breakfast was a good deal better

than he'd expected. He was mopping up the last of his eggs and kidneys with a slice from an excellent loaf of bread when Thea came in. She took in the spread at a glance. "I suspect the servants have given up their breakfast for us," she said and picked up a plate.

The post-chaise arrived right on time, and Thea surveyed it without enthusiasm as she tied her bonnet strings and gathered up her possessions.

At the front door, the housekeeper bobbed a curtsy. "If you please, ma'am... I had the footman put a hamper in the chaise for you."

"That's very thoughtful, Mrs. Wells."

"And ma'am? I do hope you won't feel it necessary to report this... event... to his lordship."

Thea lifted an eyebrow. "Shall we be coming back this way, Will?"

He tugged on his gloves. "I expect so, in a few days."

"In that case, we shall see. Won't we, Mrs. Wells?"

"Yes, ma'am. Thank you, ma'am. You won't be disappointed."

Will held back a smile as he tugged on his gloves. One thing Lord Carrington had been right about – this woman would make a formidable countess.

If she ever got the chance, of course. The reminder of their mission soured his mood, and he settled into the chaise with a sigh.

"Will today be as long as yesterday was?" Thea asked.

"Nearly, I'm afraid. I see Mrs. Wells also added some pillows. If your night's sleep was as unrefreshing as mine, you may want a nap before long."

She looked at him curiously.

"Not that I'm saying you look tired," he added hastily. "I know better than to make any such statement to a lady."

Thea laughed. "You'd be right, though. I think I've never spent a more uncomfortable night."

We could have kept each other company... and perhaps not minded that we didn't get any sleep.

That was a picture to make a tired man's head spin, so he

was grateful when Thea snuggled down into the cushions and said, "Tell me about your family. You know all about mine – such as it is – so it's only fair I know about yours. Was your father a solicitor as well?"

Will nodded. "In Southampton. He died while I was at university, or I would have gone into his practice."

"And your mother?"

"She still lives there. She has a sister nearby, and many friends."

"But you don't have brothers or sisters? She must miss you a great deal."

"I've asked her to move to London." Will smiled at the memory. "But she says when a man's mother keeps house for him, he feels no need to marry, and since she has no wish to delay me from taking that step, she refused to consider a move until –" He broke off, remembering exactly what his mother had said.

What would his mother think of Thea? The village that was their destination lay deep in the Hampshire countryside, not all that far from Southampton. If this had been a wedding trip – but it wasn't, and their business required all possible speed. Perhaps there would be another time.

"Oh, you can't stop there," Thea protested.

She *had* asked, and it would be rude not to answer. "She said she would move closer once I've started a family, because she wants to be around to see me deal with a son who's as single-minded as I am."

Thea was silent.

Only days had passed since she had made it clear that her view of their marriage did not include conjugal relations, or children. When she had said it, Will had been neither surprised nor particularly displeased, since she was no more his choice than he'd been hers.

He'd spoken the truth when he'd said her request was fair. Everything had happened so suddenly; there would be plenty of time to adjust to the idea of marriage – to the reality that they were linked together, to the exclusion of all others, forever.

He hadn't expected to feel impatience over the matter – perhaps not ever, but certainly not so soon. And yet... was he the only one to feel that things had changed quite a lot in these last few days?

"Do you want a family, Will?" The question was little more than a breath. "Even if it turns out that there's no title to pass on?"

"Of course I do. I always have. Don't you?"

"There's never been a reason for me to think about it."

"But now you must think about it. You can't just avoid the question. And it's not just up to you."

"That's why you said you'd wait *for now*."

"Yes. But not forever. We are married, and we'll always be married." His voice was sharper than he liked; he tried to soften it. "Is it Lord Carrington you're thinking of? If you're aiming to punish him by not giving him grandchildren..."

"Then I'd be punishing you, too, wouldn't I?" Her wide eyes were soft, darker than usual and filled with uncertainty. "Will, can we stop talking about it? I need to think."

"For now," he said.

She looked out the window and chewed at her lower lip. He wanted to make her stop, before the chaise hit a rut at the wrong moment and she drew blood. No, what he wanted was to haul her onto his lap and show her that consummating their marriage could be pleasurable – more than just pleasurable – for both of them.

But she had asked for time to consider, and Will prided himself on being fair, of understanding that there were always multiple ways to view a problem.

If only she would let him show her that being married didn't have to be a problem.

* * *

The village where Miss Tomlinson's aunt lived was charming, Thea thought – small and picturesque, full of cottages scattered at random around a church so old that it seemed to have grown straight out of the rocky soil that surrounded it.

Or perhaps she was so delighted simply because they had encountered no delays on the road and so they arrived by mid-afternoon, well before the hour Will had estimated when they set out.

The inn in the center of the village was small and quiet, unlike the ones where they had paused throughout the day to change horses. The baggage was unloaded; the post-chaise pulled into the yard, and in the common room Thea sank down by a table where a maid had just deposited a tea tray, grateful beyond words for a seat that didn't sway and jolt under her. "What's first?" she asked as she handed a steaming cup across to Will.

"The church – to check the parish records. If the marriage took place here, as Mr. Tomlinson insists, then it has to have been recorded in the parish books."

"I wonder if Mr. Tomlinson knows that. Was he shocked to find you're a solicitor and know these things?"

"Perhaps he didn't anticipate me, but he should have expected that Lord Carrington would immediately call in experts."

Thea frowned. "I'm not so certain of that. His lordship has made no secret of being unhappy with you. Perhaps Mr. Tomlinson heard that gossip and assumed that his lordship would be eager to embrace any alternative."

"No wonder I like being around you," Will said dryly. "You always make me feel so good about myself."

"Sorry. Just telling the truth as I see it."

"You're right, of course. If you hadn't come along and it was just me being pushed aside, I expect Lord Carrington would have been a great deal easier to convince."

Thea finished her tea and stood up.

"You're not going to indulge in these somewhat dry, tired-looking cakes?"

"No, I'll leave them all for you. I would like to wash off some road dust before we go to the church."

When she came back, feeling a bit refreshed, Will was eating fresh buttered toast. "I saved some for you."

She eyed him doubtfully but she sat down and poured herself another cup of tea. The minutes seemed to drag, though, as she nibbled. She felt restless, eager to get their investigation started. Was Will honestly hungry, or was he delaying – now that they might be so close to the truth?

"If we have luck," she pointed out, "we could have an answer by nightfall."

"You're trying to be a managing wife, aren't you?" Will reached for another slice of toast.

"Not, apparently, with any success," Thea pointed out.

He laughed, finished his toast, and stood. "Let's go."

The church was quiet and dim, with the Saturday afternoon sun only a trickle through the small windows set high in the stone walls. A middle-aged lady who was arranging flowers near the altar, getting ready for Sunday services, looked up in surprise as they came in, and Will asked for the vicar.

"He's back in the vestry," the woman said, and pointed the way.

The vicar was young, barely into his thirties. Thea thought his boyish looks might be quite popular with the ladies of the parish.

Will explained their mission. "We're seeking evidence of a marriage involving a Miss Tomlinson that may have been conducted here, some seven or eight months ago. May we look through the parish registers?"

Thea admired how carefully he had stated the question, not indicating whether they were hoping to confirm that the marriage had taken place, or prove that it hadn't happened at all.

The vicar smiled. "Oh, yes. Miss Tomlinson. I remember that one."

Thea's heart sank. She'd been telling herself the outcome wouldn't truly matter – but now she realized that like Will, she would be disappointed if Miss Tomlinson really was Lady Calvert and her baby might be the heir.

Only because of the school, she reminded herself. She hadn't turned into a grasping, selfish shrew in these few days.

She wasn't the kind of woman who would feel cheated if she didn't have the London house and the country estate and the jewels and all the trappings of wealth. But the school...

The vicar picked up a big ledger and riffled through the pages. "Here it is."

Thea and Will bent over the book, and there it was – neatly listed toward the top of the sheet. Jane Tomlinson and Robert, Lord Calvert, and a date seven months earlier – just a few weeks before Robert's death.

Not a busy parish, Thea thought, if the weddings for more than half a year had barely finished filling a single page.

"Do you remember this couple?" she asked the vicar. Her voice felt hoarse.

"This ink all looks alike," Will said. "As though everything was written at the same time. Isn't that unusual?"

The vicar looked from one of them to the other. "No, I don't recall the couple," he said, "because I've only been in the parish two months now. And these records *have* all been written at the same time."

"Why?" Thea asked. "Isn't it the usual practice to record things one at a time, as soon as they happen?"

The vicar sighed. "The man I replaced was old and feeble, and his record-keeping had become a bit helter-skelter. There were loose pages in the register, things out of order – and sometimes he scrawled his notes on bits of paper and later entered them in the parish's official ledgers. Much of that work was left undone when he died. One of my first tasks in the parish has been to get the records updated and back in order." He sounded quite proud of himself. "I added that page just a fortnight since."

Was this good news, or bad? Thea tried to catch Will's eye, but he was closely watching the vicar. "You wouldn't happen to still have the paper where this marriage was originally recorded?" Will asked.

"Of course I do. I thought better of burning the bits and pieces until I had the ledgers entirely updated, in case the bishop insisted on inspecting the originals. Not that I will volunteer to show them to him. Poor Mr. Cannon was doing his best, I'm sure, and I wouldn't like to have the bishop think badly of him." He began to scrabble around the table.

That was a lovely Christian attitude, Thea thought – but perhaps it was also a bit naive. Or was this just wishful thinking on her part?

"That one was out of order, I remember – as though he just opened the book at random and tucked it in." The vicar tugged a stack of odd sheets from under a book, licked a fingertip, and be gan sorting. "Yes, this is the one."

Will looked at the page which had been detached from an official register book, and then spread out the others from the packet.

"Every one of them looks different," Thea said. But maybe that was just because of the old vicar's failing health. It didn't mean they were looking at evidence of fraud – but how could they know for certain?

"It should be easy enough to check," the vicar said, and raised his voice. "Miss Fletcher? When you're finished with the flowers, will you come here, please?"

The woman from the church rushed in, still holding a stem of lilies. "Do you need me to do something for you right away, Father?"

She sounded eager, almost excited. Yes, Thea thought, the young vicar was definitely popular with at least this portion of the females of the parish.

"I'm sure you'll know about this marriage record," the vicar said. "Isn't Miss Tomlinson your niece?"

Thea was startled; Will was obviously not. But of course he would have known the aunt's name before embarking on this journey; she hadn't thought to ask.

"Yes." The woman's whole manner had changed. She was no longer fluttering over the vicar like a moth near a candle; instead she was watchful, wary. "What about her?"

Will took over. "Did you witness the marriage?"

"I –" Her gaze shifted and she looked around the room as if she were looking for an exit and had forgotten the door was behind her. "Of course I did."

"You must have been present," Will agreed, "since

according to this bit of paper you gave approval to an underage girl to marry, even though you didn't have the legal authority to do so."

The vicar gasped. "Miss Fletcher!"

The woman's mouth thinned to a narrow line. "That doesn't mean it wasn't a real marriage."

"Perhaps," Will said. "But the record is written on this loose page, and it doesn't look like the ones in the official register."

"Well, if that's all you're fussing about..." She sniffed. "Look through the books – you can see the mess the old vicar made of them. Anyway, I was there. You weren't. I'm finished with the flowers, Father, so I'll be going home now." She marched out.

The vicar nodded. "I'm shocked, of course, that she didn't follow the rules – it seems so unlike Miss Fletcher. But I'm sure she had her reasons. And I must say I'm not surprised that Mr. Cannon didn't check whether she was in a position to give the necessary permission."

Will tapped a finger on the loose page. "When did you first see the record of this marriage?"

"When I started assembling the events to be listed on that page. I'd sorted out all of the pieces so the entries would be in the right order in the book, but that page fell out of the ledger as I started to work that day." The vicar looked puzzled. "Surely you're not saying my predecessor was involved in something underhanded. He would never—"

"If I were you," Will said, "I'd stop rewriting the records in the official ledgers until I'd consulted with the bishop. And don't throw away any of those bits and pieces. Other people may want to inspect them."

Thea's breath was still coming in spurts, and her stomach still felt all-gone, as they walked back to the inn. The surety of loss, followed so quickly by conflicting evidence, had left her nerves in an uproar. "What did we just prove?"

"Not much. It seems certain that the previous vicar really was just an unorganized drone, too ill to care about proper record-keeping. If this was the only event to have been recorded on a loose page, it would be more suspicious. But the fact remains that the marriage is listed right there in the official registers."

"Which that naive young man admitted are a fraud!"

"Perhaps not actually a fraud, just a well-meaning mistake," Will said. "And the aunt will swear that it happened."

"Where does that leave us?" She sighed. "I know. Exactly where we were. And now?"

"I suppose we may as well travel back to London."

"I was afraid you were going to say that. I haven't stopped swaying yet from today's drive."

"But we don't need to start until morning," he said. "In the meantime, perhaps we can find some people around the village who will tell us more about Miss Fletcher."

* * *

In the next hour, Will accomplished little but to give himself a headache.

Everyone in the village seemed to like Miss Fletcher. She was friendly, they said. Always willing to help, devoted to the church, particularly fond of the new young vicar. She was the one who arranged the flowers for the altar, helped to organize the bazaars, called on sick parishioners.

Will was soon frustrated and ready to give up – though he was annoyed at himself for letting his feelings get in the way of investigating. If this had been the business of a regular client, what would he have done differently? He honestly didn't know.

Thea, who had listened patiently to his intensive questioning of the villagers, seemed to have read his mind. "She can't possibly be so perfect." She eyed him speculatively. "Perhaps you shouldn't be a solicitor."

"If you're suggesting I change my profession, Thea–"

"I just mean you have to talk to the right people in the right way. You sound too official right now, when what we really need is gossip."

He felt like growling at her. "And you're the expert there, I suppose?"

"I can't be worse at it than you are. We're going shopping, and you are going to be the put-upon husband who would much rather be in the taproom drinking ale."

"That much is quite true," Will said under his breath.

Her eyes gleamed. "Very good. Keep it up – the soft muttering, I mean. You're disgusted at how long it's taking me to find everything I want."

He waved her on and watched with reluctant interest as she chatted and toyed with ribbons while the milliner trimmed a new hat for her – a hat Will was called upon to pay for and then to carry, nestled into a sizable hat box, as they moved on through the village.

The grocer's wife seemed delighted to have a new audience for her stories, and Will acquired another package, this one containing local honey, with instructions to handle the jar carefully so the seal didn't come loose. Just down the street, the baker's wife handed over a half-dozen tarts filled with lemon curd, wrapped in a twist of brown paper, along with her succinct observations, and Will had to juggle packages to dig into his pockets when Thea imperiously held out a hand for the necessary coins.

By that time the muttering was coming naturally.

Thea seemed to be enjoying herself, though. And he had to admit he was amused by her ability to prod the village gossips into saying more than they intended. He almost forgot how important this investigation was to their future, caught up as he was in admiring her skill. She really was a puzzle, his Thea...

His Thea? Just when had he started thinking of her in that way?

But all their efforts were in vain. By the time the sun was sinking and Will was laden down with parcels, the worst thing anyone had said about Miss Fletcher was that she could be, perhaps, a bit silly. And that sometimes the sick parishioners would rather she stayed home instead of annoying them with her bland beef jelly and her inane sympathy.

In short, the woman was nothing more than she seemed – an aging spinster, caught up in her flowers and the church. She didn't fit the picture of a mastermind who was capable of dreaming up a scheme, manufacturing a record to make it seem a marriage had taken place, and taking advantage of the vicar's disorganization to sneak into the vestry and slip the forgery into the official records.

If the marriage actually was a fraud, it hadn't been Miss Fletcher's idea.

But had it been Mr. Tomlinson's? If the two had been brother and sister, he'd have been more likely to believe it. But their relationship was through Mr. Tomlinson's long-dead wife, who had been Miss Fletcher's sister.

In their private parlor at the inn, Thea sagged onto a settee by the fire. "How perfectly exhausting that was. And how perfectly useless."

Will felt like agreeing, but she already sounded so discouraged that he didn't want to make it worse. "Not entirely. You did end up with an expensive new hat."

"Add it to Lord Carrington's bill. In fact, give it to him. I will never wear it, but perhaps her ladyship might."

"Which one? Lady Carrington, or Lady Calvert?"

"If that's supposed to be a joke..."

He couldn't try any longer. "Sadly, it wasn't."

She looked at him for a long time. "You think it's hopeless, then." Her voice was heavy, lifeless.

He couldn't bear seeing her like that. "The school will be all right, Thea. His lordship can't take back his promises."

"But that bargain was based on you being his heir. If you're not, then it would be dishonest to keep everything he gave us. We'd be quite literally taking all those things from a baby – and *don't* remind me again that the child might be a girl, or I shall scream."

Will decided not to test her. So he bit his tongue instead, and thought of how very long the next few months might be – until they would know for certain.

Chapter Nine

By the time they returned to Tanner's Close late the following day, it felt to Thea as if they'd been traveling for weeks. As the post-chaise pulled into the long carriage drive, she regarded the house without enthusiasm. "I can't decide which would be worse," she mused. "Owning this place for a little while and then losing it again, or keeping it and having to face the task of getting it running properly."

"I thought you had the solution. Dismiss all the employees and start over."

"The trouble with that approach is that many of the employees most likely come from the village, and sending them all away means they'll go home and talk about it – and us. That would lead to difficult relations with all the neighbors."

Will was looking at her oddly. "How do you know so much about villages, if you've never lived in one?"

"If you're wondering if it's one of those things that's come down in my blood, it isn't," she said dryly.

"The possibility never occurred to me. Lord Carrington doesn't seem the type to fret about maintaining relations with the neighbors."

"I suspect Bedford Square isn't much different from a village. Most of our maids and kitchen helpers are girls from within a few blocks of the school. They come to work for Madame till they're trained, and then they go off to positions that pay more, and we take on another neighborhood girl and start over. But every mother in the vicinity knows all about the school and how the girls who work there are taught more than just how to clean. People talk."

She climbed down from the chaise just as the front door swung open, revealing a butler they hadn't seen at all on their last visit and a footman who ran out to help unload the baggage.

Will stopped to talk to the post-boys, giving them directions for the following day's trip back to London, but Thea went on into the house, bracing herself for another uncomfortable stay.

As she came in, however, the staff was lining up down the hallway, directed by the housekeeper who was still chivvying the youngest housemaids into line. The air carried a light tang of lemon oil, the stair rail positively gleamed, and the checkerboard marble of the floor reflected sunlight to the point it was almost painful until the closing door shut out the slanting rays.

"My goodness, Mrs. Wells," Thea said. "It appears you've been very busy."

The housekeeper curtsied. "We all have, ma'am. I just wanted to say that I take full responsibility for the disarray the house was in before. While it's true my staff had grown lazy...." She cast a disapproving eye down the line of servants. Some of them flushed and ducked their heads, embarrassed. But one young maid looked straight at Thea, her face set in resentment.

If I was staying, she thought, *that girl wouldn't be here long.*

The housekeeper was still talking. "...But I haven't been doing my job, either, by not requiring them to keep up the standards, even though it looked as if his lordship would never again be in residence. I want to assure you that will not happen again. And we – all of us – are delighted to know that you and Mr. Archer are the new owners."

Not everybody was delighted, Thea thought. Not that young maid, for one. But it didn't matter, for someone else would have to sort things out at Tanner's Close.

The thought weighed heavily on her because it had come so automatically, and she realized she'd already given up the idea of ever having something like this of her own. She wondered if Miss Tomlinson... no, she'd better get used to calling her Lady Calvert... would care about this house.

Oh, stop it, Thea – quit feeling sorry for yourself.

But the bracing order did little to change the underlying feeling, and she was still feeling blue half an hour later when she came back downstairs from a quick wash and found Will in the drawing room. The dust covers were gone, revealing furniture that looked worn but was scrupulously clean. A fire took the chill from the room, and a tea tray stood ready on the table. "You've worked a miracle here," he said.

"Doesn't this look homey?" Her voice trembled a little.

Will had heard the quaver, of course, for he looked thoughtful. "We'll work it out, Thea. We may not have to return everything to his lordship—"

She sucked in a deep breath. "I thought we talked about this."

"Stop," he said. "I agree that giving it back is the right thing to do, if it ends up that there's a new heir."

"Then what are you saying?"

"Two things. First, we have a few months before we know for certain, and that gives us time to plan a way to keep the school funded. Second – well, his lordship doesn't know we've decided to give it all back, does he? And we aren't going to tell him."

She frowned. "I don't understand."

"Things like the London house don't much matter, since it's only a lease. And the jewels he promised you are still in his safe. You were right about that, of course; it was short-sighted of me to let him keep hold of them. But I'm sure the trustees would have a few things to say to him about the way he blithely gave away property that – entailed or not – should have stayed with the holder of the title."

"You mean Tanner's Close."

"Exactly. They'll put pressure on him to get it back. But he can't just demand it, because the transfer was legally binding. He'll have to give us something in return."

"You're planning to blackmail him to keep the school in funds."

"I'd prefer to call it negotiating from a position of strength," Will said thoughtfully. "I don't know about you, but

I learned quite a lot from that last round of dealing with him."

Her smile was feeble, and she finally bit her lip to stop the wobble. He was so steady, so perfectly solid. Meanwhile, she felt off-center, as though at any moment she might start to cry. But it wasn't Tanner's Close she wanted to wail over. It wasn't even the school, though at least that would make more sense.

"I'm so sorry," she said softly. "About all of this."

"It isn't your fault, Thea."

"Even if I hadn't come along, the whole situation with Miss Tomlinson would be hanging over your head anyway. But..." Her voice wavered, and she couldn't look at him. "But it wouldn't have been so *important* then, because you wouldn't be saddled with a wife you never wanted."

He moved so quietly that she didn't realize he was standing right behind her until she felt his breath stirring her hair and the gentle weight of his hand on her shoulder as he turned her to face him.

He didn't even speak, just put his arms around her. Thea resisted for an instant – but it felt so good to be comforted, and she sank into the warmth of his body. He held her, resting his chin lightly against the top of her head.

It was important to her that he should understand what she was feeling, even though she didn't quite know why it mattered. Perhaps she felt guilty? Though she had no real reason; she had not been the one who manipulated him into this marriage. Still, if she hadn't confronted Lord Carrington, Will wouldn't be in this predicament.

"It would have been a different thing," she murmured, "with Lord Carrington's resources. It wouldn't have mattered so much because we could have gone our separate ways. But it won't be so easy to avoid each other if all we have is your chambers.... Oh! I don't even know if you can still live there if you have a wife. Is that allowed?"

"That's not something you need to worry about, Thea. Even under the worst conditions, I'll find a way to make a home for you, though it won't be as grand as the one on Bloomsbury Square."

"But you shouldn't have to, when it wasn't your choice. It's not fair. Isn't there a way to turn back the clock? To make it so we didn't actually marry?"

"Is that what you want, Thea?"

No. No, it's not.

The denial came so quickly that for a moment she was afraid she'd said it aloud – even though the quick mental response made little sense to her. Of course she'd prefer to go back to the way things had been, before she'd confronted her father and he'd turned her life, and Will's, upside down. Of course she'd rather none of this had happened.

And yet...

"Because, short of an act of Parliament, it's impossible," he said.

She told herself she should not feel the slightest thread of relief to hear that no matter what either of them would prefer, there was no way to dissolve this marriage.

"And in any case, what if I don't want to avoid you?"

Startled, she pulled back a little to look up at him.

"I'm getting rather used to having you around." He cupped her cheek in one large palm, and bent his head.

Thea's heart gave an odd little jerk. She would have pulled away, but somehow all her muscles seemed to have frozen. No, not frozen – for if that had been the case, they'd be hard and cold, and instead her body seemed to have turned to mush. Warm, bubbly mush. And her mind apparently had followed, because she couldn't seem to maintain a single coherent thought amongst all the babble.

Unlike the kiss in the hotel sitting room, this one wasn't tentative. Though his lips were soft, warm, gentle against hers, this time he wasn't asking permission. He was taking what was his. He was not demanding or forcing her. But he was claiming his rights. He was claiming *her*.

When he'd agreed that consummating their wedding could wait, he'd said *for now*. Apparently, the grace period was coming to an end.

She couldn't think, not like this. Not with him holding her close, nibbling at the corners of her mouth, at the incredibly-sensitive spot right below her ear, and then returning once again to her lips with a groan that vibrated through her. She felt so wobbly she was certain she couldn't stand on her own, but she didn't care. What was so important about standing, anyway? Perhaps she should just sink down on the floor, pulling him with her so neither of them would have to think about staying upright. Then he wouldn't have to bend so far to reach the hollow at the base of her throat, the one that sent quivers racing through her when he brushed it with his lips, and she could more easily thread her fingers through his soft dark hair.

He deepened the kiss, invading her mouth, and the taste of him called out to her. She melted against him and he pulled her even closer, the hard angles of his body hot against hers.

Someone, in what felt like a hazy distance, coughed. Thea jerked, but Will was holding her too tightly for her to pull away. He raised his head a fraction. "What is it, Wells?" She'd never heard that rough edge to his voice before.

"Your pardon, sir. I was inquiring whether you and Mrs. Archer would like the cake stand replenished."

There's a cake stand? She hadn't paid a single moment's attention to the tea tray.

"Perhaps a fresh pot of tea, my dear?" Will said.

"Yes, of course. That would be lovely. Thank you, Wells." She tried to extract herself from Will's arms, but he didn't relax, even when the butler bowed and departed. "That was embarrassing."

"It would have been worse if he'd been able to see the effect you have on me."

She considered. "Oh. Yes." What was wrong with her, anyway, that she wasn't shocked by the way his body was pressed against hers? She should be frightened by the way they fit together, how her breasts were crushed against his chest, and the intimate warmth of his erection pressing between her legs, making her feel as if her petticoat had dissolved away.

Will smiled a little and let her go. "Perhaps if we sit?"

She was relieved that he didn't move to renew his

attentions. Of course she was relieved. She needed time to think about this, time to decide what she would do.

Will was behaving as he always did – he was making the best of the situation. It was his nature to find a positive side in everything, but his attitude must also be an outgrowth of his training. Thea suspected that anyone who worked with the law had to understand that sometimes things didn't turn out in the way he wanted. Will must have learned to shrug off defeat and go on – accepting the facts and working with them, rather than railing at fate.

But perhaps his acceptance of this particular situation was also partly because he was a man. Wouldn't any man, holding any woman in that kind of intimate embrace, have reacted in the same way? Even if she wasn't the woman he would have chosen, she was his wife – and since there was no changing that, he had simply adjusted himself to the reality.

But what about Thea? Could she do the same?

* * *

Dinner at Tanner's Close was a very different event than the scratched-together meal they'd had on their first night in the house. In the dining room freshly-cleaned silver gleamed on the table against crisp white linen. Soup was followed by fish and then by beef; after that, Thea lost track.

She watched as night closed in, as shadows gathered in the corners of the big room, as candlelight transformed from a subtle, supplemental glow to the sole illumination, turning the table into an island where only she and Will existed, talking at random about nothing because the servants were always in the room.

Finally, the last course was swept away, the cloth was removed, a port decanter was set in front of Will – and Thea excused herself and retreated to the drawing room.

The housekeeper herself brought in the coffee tray. Thea must have looked puzzled, for Mrs. Wells flushed a little and said, "Your pardon, ma'am, I would have left this to Wells as usual, but you may not have time in the morning, and I just wanted to say... I wanted to apologize for the simplicity of the dinner tonight, and for getting the menu all wrong. The cook thought... But there's no value in excuses. I assure you we'll do better as we get to know your tastes, ma'am."

"There was nothing wrong with the menu." Thea fumbled for something to compliment – which was hard to do when she'd barely noticed any of the food she'd pushed around on her plate, much less recalled the way various dishes had been cooked and presented. "Please tell Cook that the beef was very tasty."

Mrs. Wells looked gratified. "It was grown here, on the estate. But you didn't seem to like the fish, or the vegetables, or the trifle."

"I just... wasn't hungry. All the traveling, you know – I'm not used to spending so many hours in a carriage." It wasn't a lie exactly, but the truth was she had barely been able to swallow.

Mrs. Wells looked unconvinced, but to Thea's relief she quietly went away.

Thea toyed with her coffee for a few minutes longer, and she'd just pushed her cup aside and stood when Will came in. "I didn't expect you," she said. "I was just going upstairs."

An instant too late, she realized that could sound like an invitation, and she felt color steal up into her face. "I mean..."

He came across the room to her, and for a moment she thought he was going to either sweep her into his arms or offer to keep her company in her room. Instead, he brushed a gentle hand over her hair and dropped a kiss on the top of her head. "Sleep well, my dear. If you can."

Startled, she stared up at him. Did he understand how unsettled she felt, how confused she was? "Oh – you mean the lumpy mattress."

He smiled. "What did you think I meant? Good night, Thea."

As a matter of fact, the lumpy mattress which had so interfered with her night's rest on their previous visit had been replaced; Mrs. Wells truly had been busy. But it made little difference to Thea, who could not get comfortable. She watched the moon rise and followed the angle of the rays for the next hour as they crept steadily across the carpet of her

157

bedroom. She felt warm, so she cracked open a window to admit the country air, cool and crisp and fragrant. Was that sharp tang the smell of honeysuckle? But puzzling out the variety of scents – so different from London air – didn't distract her for long, and it didn't make her sleepy. She could not settle.

She couldn't stop thinking about what Will had said. They couldn't turn back the clock; they couldn't get out of the marriage. Somehow, whether they were someday to be lord and lady, or always to remain a solicitor and a teacher, they would have to make this work.

She pushed back the blankets, tugged on a wrapper, and crossed the dressing room to a door that must lead into the bedroom Will was using.

And knocked.

* * *

The formality of a dinner party was one thing, Will thought. But it felt ridiculous to have more servants fluttering around the dining room than there were people sitting at the table, and being left alone after the meal to drink a glass of port in solitary state made him feel foolish. He was fairly certain Lord Carrington would loudly proclaim that Will was simply displaying his plebian upbringing, but after the last couple of weeks, Will didn't much care what his lordship thought.

If he was ever to be the master of this house, he decided as he settled into a chair beside the fire in his bedchamber, he would shake things up.

Though as he warmed a glass of brandy in the palm of his hand and inhaled its rich aroma, he had to admit his lordship's cellars had contained a treasure he hadn't expected.

And it was hardly appropriate to confuse the staff at Tanner's Close with his quixotic notions when they'd be leaving again within a few short hours – and they might well never come back.

In the short term, there wouldn't be time for another visit.

He would have to devote himself to business, to making amends to the clients who had been neglected while he focused on Lord Carrington's affairs. He couldn't simply wait for the Tomlinson situation to resolve, hoping that it would all work out in his favor. Will didn't dare risk letting clients drift away over the next few months, because if the marriage was upheld and the child was a boy, he would have a wife to support and only his own resources with which to do it.

He was a little surprised to find that he didn't feel resentful, or angry, or annoyed, or even particularly worried by the prospect. He was uneasy, of course, about whether he could provide adequately – as any sensible man would be when taking on the responsibility for a wife, and perhaps one day a family.

If Thea was willing.

His body warmed at the memory of that kiss this afternoon. It had probably been a good thing the butler had interrupted, for it had kept Will from acting on his impulse to toss his wife over his shoulder and carry her up to his bedchamber. How would she have reacted, if he'd done anything so abrupt? Would she have resisted? For a moment, he was certain, she had not only responded to his caresses, she'd been on the edge of making her own demands.

Or was that just wishful thinking?

She would never have been his choice, but as he'd grown to know her, he'd realized that there were much worse prospects when it came to marrying. Thea was level-headed, practical, pragmatic. Surely she, like him, would come to accept the reality that they were yoked together for life, and together they could make the best of it.

They were already growing to be friends. And if nothing else, the interlude this afternoon had proved there could be passion between them. There was at least a spark – and if he was careful in fanning that flame...

He didn't realize he'd drifted off until a faint sound at the dressing room door startled him. Rather than call out – and perhaps disturb Thea – he stalked over to see what a servant could possibly want at this hour. The boot boy, perhaps, trying to slip in unnoticed to perform some unnecessary task.

Instead, Thea stood in the doorway. Her hair, usually neatly confined in a bun or chignon, was wrapped into a thick dark braid that curved over her shoulder and past her pale, fragile throat. In the firelight, the chestnut looked more reddish than ever before, a powerful contrast to her neat white nightgown and pale wrapper. He'd had no idea her hair was so long, or so thick. He wanted to reach out and brush his hand against the braid and follow it down to the curve of her breast as it rose and fell in a quick, unsteady rhythm that betrayed her nerves.

He stepped back, inviting her in. "Brandy? There's plenty in the decanter but I only have one glass."

She shook her head.

"What's bothering you, Thea?"

Rather than answering, her gaze skittered past him and over to his bed, which was clearly undisturbed. "That's probably a new mattress, and far more comfortable. The one in my room has been changed, anyway, so I imagine this one has as well. You should try it."

Only if you'll join me.

His body tightened uncomfortably, and he tried to tamp down the mental image of them tangled together in his bed. Of her hair flowing across his pillow as he explored every inch of her skin to see if it was all as delicate, as soft, as smooth as her throat had been when he kissed her this afternoon.

He tried to regain control, and humor. "Somehow I doubt you came to discuss my mattress."

Her face flamed. "Well, no. Not exactly."

He raised an eyebrow and waited.

She toyed with the tie at the throat of her nightdress. He knew she wasn't being deliberately seductive – hell, she didn't know how! – but the tentative gesture drove him mad anyway.

"When a woman comes to a man's bedroom in her nightdress, there's usually only one reason. So if that's not why you're here, Thea, I suggest you say so quickly before I get the wrong idea."

"It wouldn't... exactly... be the wrong idea," she whispered.

He couldn't help himself, and he couldn't keep his distance. He watched as she worried the narrow ribbon between her fingers, and swallowed hard, trying not to let himself want to tug at that demure little bow so he could investigate the gentle curves of her breasts. If he so much as touched that tie, or the silken skin under it, he would not stop.

But there were other ways to accomplish the goal. He reached out to close his hand over hers, and tugged – and her fingers, still clutching the ribbon, pulled it loose.

He half-expected she would jerk away, or scramble to fix the bow, or at least squeak in shock. But she didn't.

Her scent tugged at his senses – that same drift of country flowers that had intrigued him on the day they met at the Carringtons' front door. But now it was more like a drug, undermining his common sense and pulling him down into a whirlpool of sensation.

"You are my wife," he said huskily.

For an instant, the world seemed to hang in the balance, and then she nodded, her face solemn. "Yes."

The word was far more than just a statement of fact – at least, Will hoped it was. He moved slowly, raising his hand to brush her cheek, and when she didn't pull away, he let his fingers slide to the back of her neck to draw her closer.

She tipped her face up to his. He kissed her, long and gently, and Thea sighed and nestled against him.

She was so soft, so trusting, so innocent. He must not rush her, or overwhelm her. He would take her back to her room, where she would be more at ease...

Then she opened her mouth under his and very tentatively touched her tongue to his lower lip, and his good intentions, along with his common sense, combusted. The next kiss was hot and deep and demanding, and he molded her even closer so she could feel what she was doing to him.

She pulled back a fraction, and he cursed himself as a fool for frightening her. So much for treating her carefully, for taking all the time she needed. He would deserve it, right now, if she slapped him and stormed off to her room.

But she didn't look frightened. She looked a bit startled, perhaps even puzzled, and very, very alluring. Her lips were swollen from his kiss, her eyes wide, her pupils dark...

"Is that how married people kiss?" she whispered.

"If they're very fortunate." Will was having trouble getting his breath.

"It doesn't seem quite..."

"Proper? Anything can be proper, between a husband and wife, so long as they agree."

"Oh." She looked thoughtful, and then she said, "I was thinking it didn't seem to be quite enough."

Will tried not to laugh. But between sheer relief that he hadn't ruined everything after all and amusement that his Thea was still the same unpredictable creature, he couldn't help it.

* * *

He was holding her so closely that she felt as well as heard his laugh. The vibrations rumbled through her body, setting off tremors. "If you're going to laugh at me," she said crossly, "then you should let me go."

"I'm not. Not laughing at you, and not letting you go." He smiled down at her, his eyes alight. "Thea, you're a breath of fresh air." He picked her up and in two steps was beside the bed. Awkwardly, with one hand, he dragged the blankets back, laid her down, and simply stood there looking down at her for an instant. "Are you sure about this?"

Annoyed, she said, "Aren't you? You don't sound like it."

"Am I certain I want to make love to you? Oh, yes. But if you still want to wait..."

"How can I be sure about anything when I have no idea what... I mean..." She felt herself color, and it was a struggle not to stammer. "Will, I don't want to think any more."

A smile tugged at his lips. "I can help you with that," he murmured, and then he was beside her, his mouth once more hot against hers. Not demanding this time, but gently giving and taking, nipping and caressing. For a long time all he did was kiss her, and only after she sighed and arched against him did he let his palm slide over her cheek and along the edge of her throat, over her shoulder and down the length of her arm. His fingertips drifted across her stomach, under the edge of her wrapper.

The heat of his mouth seemed to melt her bones, and when the heat of his hand brushed the underside of her breast, seeming to burn away the thin fabric of her nightdress, she gasped a little. He went still, his palm not quite cupping her breast, and after a moment her body seemed to surge of its own will, pushing against his hand. A spark lit in his eyes, and he moved again, his thumb gently brushing her nipple till it peaked. How could such a gentle touch cause a tug that she felt all the way to her core?

The room was dim, lit only by the candles beside his chair next to the fire. But her eyes had adjusted till she had no trouble seeing the planes of his face, the ripple and play of muscles in his chest and arms... just when had he disposed of his dressing gown?

"Don't think," he whispered. She considered telling him that no matter what her wishes, and no matter what he might do, she simply wouldn't be able to turn off the process entirely – but he moved just enough to take her nipple into his mouth. As the thin fabric seemed to disappear, her mind went to mush again as primitive desire shot straight through her.

"Such a passionate creature," he murmured, and the vibration of his voice against her breast sent her soaring. "But let's get rid of this nightdress."

It seemed to her that he already had, because surely she could feel his warmth just as strongly as if there had been nothing between them. Still, if it would make him happy...

Dimly, she wondered why she cared so much about him being pleased. But she'd think about that some other time.

Feeling awkward, not knowing how to move, she tried to help – and finally it was done and she lay bared to his gaze.

She felt shy, and her instinct was to cover herself – but as she reached for the sheet, he captured her hands again. "Don't," he said. "You're too beautiful to hide." He kissed her until she forgot everything except the strange sensations churning deep inside her.

The roughness of his chest hair against her breasts had made her nipples even more sensitive, so the touch of his tongue there brought her instantly to attention. He sucked gently, swirling his tongue around the aureole, while his hand slid slowly – as if accidentally – down across her belly, toying with her hip for a moment, then trailing slowly across to the soft down between her legs. She startled as he touched her and cupped her mound.

Slowly, he caressed her, and she felt an embarrassing rush of heat. "It's all right," he murmured, and she forced herself to relax as he stroked her and then slipped a fingertip inside her. "So lovely," he said. "So wet for me. Not quite ready yet... but soon."

He returned to kissing her, mimicking with his tongue the movements of his hand, until her breath tightened and quickened. He touched a tender fingertip to the sensitive nub inside her and she gasped against his mouth, half-frightened and half-astounded, as her body shattered.

He held her gently as she shuddered and quaked, and while she was still floating, he positioned himself over her and pressed himself home. She felt herself stretching to accommodate an unfamiliar intrusion that somehow felt so very right. There was an instant of pain, and then he was moving slowly inside her. His body caressed hers, rhythmic strokes soothing an ache she'd never dreamed of, and sending her soaring once more just as he cried out and spilled his seed inside her.

* * *

When Will could almost think clearly again, he was a little ashamed of himself. She was so innocent, yet so responsive, that his good intentions had gone out the window. So much for taking all the time she needed, of making her first experience so wonderful that she would fall in love with lovemaking, as well as with him...

Wait. *Love*? That must be just another example of how his mind wasn't functioning correctly.

He settled himself beside her and drew her comfortably into his arms, nestling her against his side. "Next time will be better," he murmured into her hair.

She tensed. "I'm sorry if I didn't... I don't know how to..."

He smiled and kissed her. "That's not at all what I meant. You were perfect. Next time I'll have better control of myself."

She was quiet for a while, and then very softly she said, "It's not supposed to be so ... wild?"

The question sent desire humming through his veins, and his body responded with alacrity. He had to sternly remind himself that she was inexperienced, and he must give her some time to recover before he made love to her again.

It had been clear from the beginning that Thea had strong feelings about many things, but if Will had realized how that could translate into passion in their marriage bed, he might not have been so amenable to waiting.

Still, delaying a few days – and spending this time alone together – had let them build up a sense of trust, and that had definitely been worth the wait.

"Making love can be whatever you want," he said.

She turned in his arms so they lay face to face, her breasts brushing his chest, his cock hot against her belly. He thought she blushed a little, but the firelight and the guttering candles didn't let him see for certain. "But I don't know what I want. Will you show me?"

Will's resolution to be patient, to be gentle, to wait for her to be entirely ready, went up in flames – and he was lost.

Chapter Ten

They got a very late start, because when Thea woke up in Will's arms with her back pressed against his chest, there had been an insistent part of him snuggled between her legs. He wasn't doing anything, and when she raised an eyebrow at him – thinking as she did so that her innocence was rapidly vanishing – he said, "Sorry about that. It happens. We don't need to do anything about it."

But he looked a little disappointed as she moved away and studied him, and his shaft twitched a little. "That doesn't look comfortable," she mused.

She wondered why her mother, during that awkward long-ago conversation about what men and women did together, hadn't said anything about this ... this seemingly-insatiable reaction.

Though she supposed it wasn't quite fair to blame Will for the way he seemed to spring to attention whenever she moved, when her own body apparently felt the same draw toward him, along with an odd emptiness and heat and longing that was so incredibly disconcerting she couldn't even reason out why.

"If you keep doing that," Will said dryly, "you'll be flat on your back in another half a minute."

"Doing what?" Thea realized her distraction had been so great she hadn't even realized she'd reached out a fingertip to stroke that most interesting part of him. "Oh. *That*. Do you want me to stop?"

"Hell, no," he said roughly, and pushed her knees apart. Instead of joining with her, however, he hovered over her, just looking at her most private parts. She wriggled uncomfortably, embarrassed by his stare, and he laughed, slid a thumb casually through her curls, and bent his head to lick at her center.

"What are you do – Oh!"

He flicked his tongue against her sensitive nub and said indistinctly, "I hope I'm driving you as crazy as you're making me."

His voice vibrated through her. She writhed, trying – without much conviction – to get away. But he clamped his hands gently on her thighs to hold her down and set about exploring until she bit the corner of her pillow to keep from screaming as she came. He slid deep inside her while she was still quaking, and took his pleasure just as quickly, finishing with a groan as she convulsed once more around him.

***

The post-boys were waiting, not very patiently, when they finally surfaced, and Will thought the delay was probably going to cost him extra. Not that he minded.

Breakfast had been sketchy because of their rush, and when Thea came out to the chaise, where the post-boys were strapping the luggage in place, she was carrying a slice of bread and butter. The housekeeper came bustling up with a basket, rattling some nonsense about hoping this stay had been more pleasant. Thea caught Will's eye and smiled, and he considered sending the chaise back to the village to wait a little longer. Or perhaps a great deal longer.

"Very pleasant, thank you, Mrs. Wells," Thea was saying. "The beds were far more inviting... Ah..."

Will saw the second she heard what she'd said. She turned a delightful shade of pink and hastily took another bite of her bread and butter – no doubt feeling if she had food in her mouth she couldn't put her foot in it.

Soon enough they were settled and the chaise moved off down the long carriage drive. Thea looked back, almost longingly, as they rounded a gentle curve where huge old trees cut off the view of the manor.

"Not feeling quite so reluctant about the country house now?"

She sighed. "It *would* be lovely to have a place to get out of the city in the summer." She settled back in her seat. "I've been thinking, Will."

"But you said you didn't want to do that anymore," he said mildly, just to see the reaction.

She gave him a sideways look and went straight on. "If we give up the London house…"

"Six-month lease," he reminded.

"Even though we haven't quite moved in?"

"By now I expect Madame will have transported your remaining possessions, and my man will have done the same."

"But we should tell Madame right away so when she's setting up the school, she can plan for a space for us. A couple of rooms, at least. If we had a sitting room of our own…"

"Thea." What was she babbling about? "Why would you assume we'll live at the school?"

"If we can't afford the house…"

"Not that house, no, but there will have to be a house. I will not live in a couple of rooms, surrounded by chattering schoolgirls." Deliberately, Will softened his tone. "I'm not the sort of husband who demands instant, unquestioning obedience, my dear. But I will not live under my wife's foot, either."

She chewed her bottom lip. He wanted – badly wanted – to pull her onto his lap and kiss her senseless, if only to stop her abusing one of his favorite parts of her.

She sighed, finally, and looked out the carriage window. "I just wish we knew."

"It can't be more than a couple of months until Lady Calvert's baby is born – probably less. And that time will go by quickly."

"That's why I think we should plan right now."

"And *I* think you should stop fretting."

"But it wouldn't be the worst thing, would it, Will? I know we'd have a lot less money. But we'd also not have to answer to Lord Carrington all the time."

He decided not to remind her that even if the child was a boy, Will would still be in line as the next heir, should something happen to that child before he had grown up, married, and sired a family of his own. That kind of uncertainty would make waiting for a babe to be born seem like nothing at all.

"There would be advantages," he admitted. "But would you really rather things turned out that way?"

She looked conflicted. "Does it make any sense if I say I didn't let myself think about everything that was involved, until it seemed likely it wouldn't come to that? But you really want it all, don't you?"

I already have everything I want.

The thought was so instantaneous, so clear, that he had to bite his tongue to keep himself from saying it. But it wasn't true. It couldn't be true.

Could it?

* * *

Thea had tried to nap in the chaise, but the jolting kept her from resting comfortably even though she was leaning against Will with his arm braced around her. By the time they reached Bloomsbury Square at mid-afternoon, Thea wanted nothing more than to crawl into a bed, drink a cup of tea, and go to sleep, in the hope that when she woke she'd have stopped swaying.

But Fenton stepped forward with a bow to present a silver tray bearing a folded message with Will's name on the outside. Thea had seen enough of the harsh, spiky handwriting to recognize Lord Carrington's fist.

Without hurry, Will unfolded the sheet and perused the contents. "We are summoned to Grosvenor Square," he said calmly.

No doubt to report the results of their trip – such as they were – to Lord Carrington. "Both of us?"

"We are to call on his lordship at our earliest convenience. I can make your excuses, if you like."

Thea considered, and shook her head. "No. I should be there for this conversation. But I would like to freshen up and change my dress first."

"Take your time. I have no doubt he will find fault with both our timing and our appearance no matter when we arrive."

She paused at the base of the stairway to look over her shoulder. Will was still standing in the hallway, once more studying the message from his lordship. "Aren't you coming up too?"

He smiled lazily. "Better not, or we might not get to Grosvenor Square until tomorrow."

Thea felt her blood heat, and she didn't trust herself to answer. When she noticed a footman trying in vain to stifle a snicker, she felt even more color rising in her face – she must look like a plum by now! – and rushed up the stairs, arriving at the top out of breath and feeling distinctly light-headed.

What was wrong with her, that a look, a smile, a suggestive comment from Will could make her forget everything else? She should have kept her dignity and asked the butler to send up a maid to help her change. She reached for the bell pull just as a tap sounded on the bedroom door and a young maid looked in. "Ma'am? Mrs. Fenton asked me to fill in, since Alice is next door at the school. I used to take care of the young ladies sometimes when their own maids had an afternoon out. I'm Sarah."

"Very thoughtful of her," Thea managed.

Sarah was ruthlessly efficient, and within a few minutes Thea was washed, brushed, wearing a clean, though drab, walking dress, and back downstairs where Will seemed to have magically shed the dust of the road himself.

How was it that this neat-as-a-pin, serious-looking man was the same one who just last night had showed her an entirely new side not only of him but of her? Just looking at him now, after a bare few minutes apart from him, made her heart jolt and heat blossom deep in her core.

It wasn't *comfortable* to feel this way about one's husband, but perhaps it would go away soon – when the newness had worn off and she'd grown accustomed to having him nearby. She couldn't believe that most women had this sort of reaction to the men they had married.

He looked up and smiled, and her insides melted. Perhaps she didn't want to be comfortable, she decided. Perhaps she didn't want to be like those other women. Perhaps she was the fortunate one, to have fallen in love with the man she had almost-accidentally married.

Shocked at the sudden realization, she stumbled over nothing, tried to catch herself with a hand on Will's arm, and ended up swept safely into his embrace. "Eager to see me?" he whispered in her ear, and the footman on duty at the door studiously looked at the ceiling.

Thea gathered up the frayed shreds of her composure. "Only eager to have this appointment behind us," she said as coolly as she could.

Without seeming in the least hurried, Will dropped a kiss just below her ear, where the ribbon of her bonnet didn't quite hide an exquisitely-sensitive spot. Slowly, he released her, making sure she was steady on her feet.

She wanted nothing more than to fling herself back in his arms and beg him to hold her, protect her, keep her safe. She trusted him as she had never trusted anyone else in her life – not even her mother, or Madame.

Thoughtfully, still trying to puzzle out the nature of love – and not remotely ready to think about what she was going to do about this new revelation – she took his arm and went out to the street to the waiting cab.

* * *

Grosvenor Square was unusually full of traffic, and the hackney had to maneuver slowly through the crush before it could finally pull up in front of Lord Carrington's house.

Thea had been very quiet throughout the drive, reacting to Will's occasional comments only with a distracted look that said she was barely listening.

He understood, of course; he wasn't certain he'd made sense anyway, since his thoughts, too, were focused on the reason for this summons. Was Lord Carrington simply impatient to hear what they'd discovered, or had something happened while they were gone to change the *status quo*?

Will knew fretting did no good, of course, but there had been only a few moments since he'd first seen Lord Carrington's message in which his mind *hadn't* been running in circles, and all of them had to do with Thea. First that innocent suggestion that he come upstairs with her, and then her near-fall and the excuse it offered to hold her close, to bask in her scent and her warmth.

He really must ask which flower it was which provided her perfume.

He climbed down from the cab, turning to help Thea, and stopped in his tracks at the unexpected sight of Lady Stone and her companion climbing the steps to the Carrington house.

Thea, too, paused, frowning a little. "It *shouldn't* seem odd," she said quietly. "They're on visiting terms, and her ladyship invited the Carringtons to her dinner party. But this looks more like a condolence call."

Lady Stone called out, "Oh, good, the travelers have returned. Have you, too, been summoned to take tea with Lady Carrington?"

"Definitely odd," Will said under his breath, and followed Thea up the stairs and into the entry where Jenkins stood by the open door.

"I do not have that pleasure," Thea said.

"Oh, well, come along anyway." Lady Stone waved a hand. "Penelope needs to get over her prejudice against you, and that will never happen if she's allowed to keep her distance."

Thea shot him a half-panicked look, but Will had to admit Lady Stone had a point – and at any rate, before either of them could argue, Jenkins opened the drawing room door and practically shooed all the ladies inside.

Left standing in the hall, still holding his hat and stick, Will couldn't help but hear Lady Carrington's triumphant voice. "Do come in, Lucinda," she said, "and meet Lady Calvert. My Robert's widow, you know – and soon to be the mother of Lord Carrington's heir."

* * *

Will felt as though time had collapsed, for once more he stood on the Axminster carpet in Lord Carrington's book room – just as he had on that day only a fortnight ago, when he'd still been looking for Anna Winslow and his lordship had sat behind his desk and harangued him in much the same way he was doing now.

The sensation was strange, for though this instant felt the same, so many other things had changed in that span of days. He'd met Thea. He'd been – it seemed – ousted from his role as his lordship's heir. He'd come to realize he hadn't been as reluctant to fill those shoes as he'd thought he was. And most importantly, he'd fallen in love.

No. That's impossible.

He'd also apparently lost his ability to focus, since he had hardly heard his lordship. Something about Lady Carrington having lost her mind?

Finally he interrupted. "Perhaps you should start from the beginning, sir. I gather Lady Carrington has invited Miss Tomlinson to tea?"

Lord Carrington glowered. "She's done a sight more than that. I came home from my club last night to find she's moved the damned chit into my house."

"Miss Tomlinson?"

"Are there any *other* ill-begotten females standing in line claiming to be carrying Robert's child?"

"Sorry, sir. I was taken aback."

"Get your head on straight, Archer."

"I presume you told Lady Carrington that you did not wish to house this … young person… under your roof?"

His lordship nodded. "Oh, I made myself clear. It's the most words we've said to each other in years."

"Yet Miss Tomlinson is still here." He wanted to fling his lordship's own advice back in his face. *Just tell the girl she'll have to do without.*

No, better not.

"Her ladyship is not only convinced, she's willing to tell the world. The best I could do was order them out of the city. They'll be going to Monkscroft tomorrow. In the meantime, I could hardly have the chit packed up and thrown out."

Why not? It's not like you care what anyone thinks.

But the hesitation made sense, when Will considered. "As

long as there's even the slightest chance she's telling the truth, you can't turn her away." He took a deep breath. "About that, sir...."

Lord Carrington eyed him with disfavor. "Bad news, eh?"

"There is a marriage record in the church. But there is also reason to question the legitimacy of that record." Will recited the facts, keeping his voice level.

"You think there's enough cause for doubt that Tomlinson can't just make his claim, he has to prove it?"

"I believe that's the case, sir. The anomalies, as well as the fact that the vicar who supposedly performed the ceremony cannot testify, shift the burden to the Tomlinsons to prove the ceremony did happen, rather than us having to prove it didn't. And that means the outcome will have to be decided by a court."

Lord Carrington thoughtfully chewed the end of a pen. "That'll take forever."

"Of course it could end as a moot point, if the child is a girl or doesn't thrive." Will heard the coldness in his voice and cringed. "Not that I wish for any such thing. I'm merely stating facts."

"And here I was starting to think you might shape up to be a decent peer after all."

"With Thea cracking the whip?" Will said dryly.

"Actually, that's not what I meant. But now that you've mentioned Thea, didn't you bring her?"

A commotion in the hallway distracted Will. "She came with me, sir, but Lady Stone took her in to tea with Lady Carrington. They seem to have finished, however. Do you wish to talk to her?" *Maybe explain what happened between you and her mother? – besides the obvious, of course.*

His lordship shrugged. "What do I care? Have you got her with child yet, do you think? I still want grand-children, you know."

The sheer crassness of the question set Will's hair on end.

Thea had an excellent point in not wanting to be beholden to this man for anything. For the first time, he found himself hoping that perhaps, after all, they could escape.

* * *

"Come and meet Lady Calvert. My Robert's widow, you know." Lady Carrington's voice rasped against Thea's ears.

How was it possible the woman could sound both domineering and fawning at the same time?

Lady Stone swept across the room. "So you've decided to rejoin the world and receive callers, Penelope. What a surprise it is, though, to find that Miss Tomlinson is appearing in public at all, considering her ... circum-stances."

Lady Carrington's voice was frosty. "Please give her the proper title, Lucinda. Of course this *isn't* public, and we aren't truly receiving callers. Just a few good friends to take tea. I hope that once you know her, you'll agree to take my girl under your protection. Perhaps consider *her* as a goddaughter. If you can do such a thing for that young person his lordship seems to favor, then why not... Oh, Mrs. Archer. I didn't see you there." Her voice had gone suddenly saccharine.

Thea made her curtsy, but she was fairly sure Lady Carrington had already dismissed her entirely in the flurry of the parlor maid delivering a tea tray.

"I'll give it some thought," Lady Stone said dryly. "But there's no hurry, since she's both in mourning and in confinement."

"Well, there *is* a hurry, in a sense. I did so want you to meet her before we leave. We'll be off to the country tomorrow, and we'll stay there for the rest of her mourning period – and on through the winter, I expect, settling his young lordship into the nursery. We won't be back in town until the start of the Season next spring, when she can appear in society again."

"Carrington agreed to make a lengthy stay in the country?" Lady Stone sounded curious.

"No, he'll remain in town for a while, and then who knows what his plans will be. It will be just the two of us at Monkscroft." Lady Carrington patted Miss Tomlinson's hand.

Thea suspected his lordship's decision reflected a decided wish not to be cooped up in the country with his wife and this would-be daughter-in-law. In fact, she would have bet every last one of the jewels she might technically own but had never seen.

"You may pour, Miss Harper." Lady Carrington made it sound as though she was conferring a great honor on Lady Stone's companion, rather than putting the help to work. "We're so looking forward to the quiet, aren't we, my dear?"

Miss Tomlinson, who hadn't said a single word since Thea had come into the room, looked a bit green. Was she still at the point in her pregnancy of regularly casting up her accounts? Perhaps it was just that the room was over-warm and the air felt not only stagnant but far too heavily scented. The dimness made it seem even more close. Thea was feeling a little nauseous herself; she longed to pull back the heavy draperies and throw open the windows.

Lady Carrington was still patting, and she hadn't taken her gaze off the young woman by her side. "We'll have a lovely opportunity to become friends, won't we, with only each other to depend on? I plan to watch over you *very* closely, my dear, to be certain that our baby arrives healthy and strong."

Our baby? Was the woman mad?

Miss Tomlinson jerked a little, as if the phrase grated on her as well.

Lady Stone's gaze rested thoughtfully on the girl, though she addressed Lady Carrington. "How wonderful for you, Penelope. It will be quite like having Robert back, I'm sure, to have a second opportunity to mold the heir to your standards."

Miss Tomlinson was looking seriously ill. Thea was tempted to move a little further from the girl, just in case. It would be interesting to see Lady Carrington's reaction if her Persian carpet ended up decorated with whatever Miss Tomlinson had eaten today.

Still, she couldn't help but feel sympathetic. "Perhaps some fresh air would help?" she murmured. "We could take a stroll through Grosvenor Gardens."

And perhaps I can find an opportunity to ask some leading questions.

Miss Harper approached with a cup and saucer in each

hand, for Thea and Miss Tomlinson. "That's hardly an inviting prospect. The square was very busy when we came, and now that the weather is warmer, the *smells*..." She shuddered artistically.

"I'm sure it's quieter by now," Thea said. "And surely the garden would be more pleasant than walking along the street. Flowers and trees and perhaps a bit of a breeze. Doesn't that sound inviting, Miss Tom... I mean..." Try as she might, she couldn't get her tongue to fit around the title.

Miss Tomlinson shook her head a little.

"And there was a man lurking across the way, as well," Miss Harper said. "We noticed him as we came in. I wanted to notify the watch, but Lady Stone said he was some kind of a soldier and probably harmless. Still, he was just *there* – staring at the houses."

Miss Tomlinson's eyes grew wide.

"There's no need to be afraid," Thea soothed. "There are many innocent reasons for lingering in a garden on a pleasant day."

"But not for staring," Miss Harper murmured.

"Perhaps he was admiring the architecture," Thea said briskly. "He's no doubt gone by now. It will be perfectly safe."

"I *would* like a walk," Miss Tomlinson said abruptly, and set her cup and saucer down with a crash. "Let's go right now."

"Oh, I don't think that's a good idea," Lady Carrington announced. "City air, and noise, and confusion – not at all good for our little one, you know. You need peace and quiet, and you'll soon get it. We'll have to make our journey very slowly – it will take probably five or six days on the road, in all – but you'll have me to look after you, and once we're in the country, we can focus on keeping you completely at peace."

"Or bored out of your mind," Miss Harper said under her breath.

"I want a *walk*," Miss Tomlinson said. Her voice was high and shrill and tense.

If she had been one of the young ladies at Madame's school, Thea would have given her a sharp set-down. But since

Miss Tomlinson was not her pupil, she only lifted her eyebrows and stared at the girl.

Miss Tomlinson ducked her head. "Please," she said. "I really *need* to go for a walk."

"Of course you do," Lady Stone said cheerfully. "You needn't come, Penelope, if you think the open air is too much for you."

Lady Carrington fluttered a little. "Well, I suppose if you insist on going out, my dear, of course I'll come. I couldn't dream of sending my delicate flower out, in her condition, without a proper chaperone to keep her safe."

Lady Stone gave her gravelly laugh. "Careful, Penelope, you'll hurt my feelings."

"I wasn't objecting to *you*, Lucinda." Lady Carrington eyed Thea with distaste.

Gathering bonnets and wraps for the five ladies took an inordinate amount of time, with Lady Carrington deliberating her choices at such a glacial pace that Thea was fairly sure she was delaying in the hope that everyone would give up the idea. Or possibly until the sun set.

Each time her maid brought a bonnet and Lady Carrington tied her ribbons, the well-trained footman opened the door and they all trooped over in a line, ready to go out. Then her ladyship would shake her head, pull off the bonnet, and send her maid after another, while Jenkins closed the door.

When her ladyship set about tying the fourth bonnet, Miss Tomlinson quivered like a racehorse and bolted the instant Jenkins pulled the door open.

"And there she goes," Lady Stone said thoughtfully. Her gaze slide from Thea to Miss Harper, and she gestured toward the street.

Lady Carrington swung around and called, "My dear! One simply *cannot–*"

Thea didn't hear any more, for she was already outside. Miss Tomlinson, with half a minute's head start, had plunged across the street under the very noses of a pair of grays pulling a curricle. The horses reared, the driver shouted, and the light carriage slewed sideways into a barouche which was pulling up next door, shattering a wheel.

"That was Lady Armbruster's barouche." Miss Harper's voice was dire.

Thea didn't bother to assess the accident. She was gazing across the street to the edge of the garden, where Miss Tomlinson was clasped in the arms of a tall young man in a dark green coat.

"Miss Harper, please tell my husband he's needed out here," she said, and without waiting for an answer she began to pick her way through the mayhem in the street to reach the garden.

She didn't bother with a stealthy approach, because it appeared Miss Tomlinson wouldn't notice anything short of an explosion directly under her nose. But she did halt on the far side of a large bush, far enough away to seem polite but still close enough to hear, with a little effort, what the couple were saying.

Will called, "Thea? Thea! Where are you?"

She waved impatiently, and within a minute, Will rushed up. "Are you hurt?"

"Of course not." She pointed around the bush. "I'm eavesdropping on... well, I'd call it a conversation, but it's a bit too incoherent to deserve the name. I didn't want to actually interrupt Miss Tomlinson and her... friend."

Will peeked around the bush. "I see."

"There's been quite a lot of *Oh, I so hoped it was you!* And *I thought you were gone forever!* And *I would never leave you, my love.* And *But how did you find me?*"

After a minute, Will said, "The young people seem attached to each other. I hate to interrupt them, but I would like to know—"

Lady Carrington stormed past, with Lady Stone and Miss Harper in her wake. She seized Miss Tomlinson's arm and gave her a good shaking. "Stop this nonsense at once, young lady. People are *staring*. You cannot possibly be seen with a man, in your situation. What are you thinking?"

Miss Tomlinson tried to pull away. "What I'm *thinking* is that I've had enough of you, you cow. Don't you understand?

This is the man I love!" She pressed herself even closer against the young man. "You won't leave me, Jamie?"

"Never," he murmured. "I've been here all day, hoping to talk to you – or at least get a glimpse."

"I was right," Miss Harper murmured. "He *was* lurking in the garden."

"But how did you know where to look?" Miss Tomlinson asked.

Will muttered, "I'd like to hear that myself."

Thea stared at him. With so many unanswered questions, *that* was the one he chose to wonder about? She could think of a half-dozen ways, beginning with the maids in Mr. Tomlinson's house. They would no doubt have a good idea about where his daughter had gone. And if the builder talked to his servants in anything like the way he generally behaved, they would hardly feel loyal enough to keep secrets.

Will stepped forward. "Let's all step inside so we can sort this out."

Miss Tomlinson looked at him as if his hair was on fire. "Go back inside that house so they can lock me up again? Not hardly."

"I assure you that will not happen, Miss Tomlinson... and I gather it *is* Miss Tomlinson? Though perhaps it is Mrs..." He tipped his head inquiringly at the young man. "Your name, sir?"

"Lieutenant James McFarland," the young man said. "And no, we're not wed. Not yet."

"But you *will* marry me, won't you, Jamie?" Miss Tomlinson pleaded.

"Of course, love. As soon as we can manage it."

Lady Carrington sputtered, "She can't possibly marry while she's in mourning for my son!"

Lady Stone took her arm. "Penelope," she said patiently, "the one thing we seem to have established so far is that she is not, and has never been, Lady Calvert. Am I correct, young woman?"

Miss Tomlinson nodded. "And thank heaven for that!"

Will surveyed the young couple. "We need to clear up all

the questions about how this happened. I give you my personal assurance that if you come inside and share the details, I will do everything in my power to assure that you will be able to marry promptly. I'm assuming Mr. Tomlinson did not approve of your match?"

"He detests the idea of his daughter marrying a soldier," the young man said. "He refused his permission, and then I was posted off to Northumberland and couldn't get leave to come back for my darling when she found herself in a delicate situation." He looked tenderly down into Miss Tomlinson's face. "I believe we should answer the questions as best we can, my dear. There are a few I'd like to ask myself – like how you came to be here at all."

They made quite a procession as they paraded across the street, where the disabled carriages still blocked traffic.

The Carringtons' front door stood open, with Jenkins – his training forgotten – staring in amazement and blocking the way. But at the base of the steps, Miss Tomlinson balked and shook her head. "I won't. I've had enough of that place."

"Take them to my house," Lady Stone suggested.

Miss Tomlinson shivered and clung to her young man. "I don't want to go anywhere."

"It's either that or air your business in public," Thea said firmly. There was no answer. She shrugged. "Then I suppose we talk about it right here."

Just a few feet away, the aristocratic owner of the crippled barouche, still firmly in her seat even though the broken wheel had tilted the vehicle at an acute angle, had raised her quizzing glass to take in the entire scene. "Penelope Carrington?" she rasped. "Is that you? What on earth is going on here?"

"That's what I'd like to know," boomed Lord Carrington as he pushed Jenkins aside and strode down the steps.

The grooms and drivers, who had been working to separate their disabled vehicles and soothe the high-strung horses, paused to watch the unfolding scene instead.

Lady Carrington whimpered.

Miss Tomlinson cringed away from Lord Carrington as she

181

tried to hide behind her young man, and it took all of Will's skills to draw her out. Even then, she pleaded ignorance. She insisted she didn't know how the scam had come about, or why, or how it had been accomplished – only that it had all been her father's idea.

"I was just waiting for Jamie to come back and marry me, but when my father found out about the baby, he was *so* angry. He told me Jamie was gone for good and I'd be ruined – but if I could convince his lordship, I could be rich and live in a grand house. Much he knew about what it would be like!" She glared at Lady Carrington. "Oh, and I heard him telling Aunt Fletcher that all she had to do was slip the papers into the right spot in the parish books. She said she didn't want to, but he reminded her of all the bills he's paid for her." She shrugged. "That's all I know. Can I go now?"

"I should call the Runners and charge you with fraud." Lord Carrington looked down his nose at her, but addressed Lieutenant McFarland. "Take this young woman out of my sight immediately, and be certain that I never encounter her again. She's nothing to do with me and mine."

Will gestured to the young man and stepped aside for a low-voiced exchange. Thea looked around at the crowd they'd gathered. Half of Grosvenor Square must have come out to see the performance. She noted whispers and nudges, alongside looks of puzzlement, disgust, excitement. More than a few people seemed to be suppressing enjoyment. She must not be the only one who found Lady Carrington difficult to deal with.

But just now her ladyship looked lost, hurt beyond bearing – almost as though she had shrunk in the last few minutes.

Thea didn't want to feel sympathetic, but she couldn't help it. *This must be like losing her son all over again.* She put a gentle hand on Lady Carrington's arm. "Let me take you inside, my lady."

Lady Carrington violently pulled away. "I don't need help from the likes of you!" she spat.

Stunned, Thea stood frozen.

"Now, Penelope," Lady Stone said firmly. "There has been pain aplenty as it is. Don't make things even worse."

Will waved off the young couple, who started down the street, and came back to the group at the foot of the stairs. "Lady Carrington," he said, and there was something in his voice which made the woman stop with one foot on the step and half-turn toward him. "Ma'am, you will not treat my wife this way."

"Well, how about that," Lord Carrington said. "Maybe you'll grow a backbone someday after all, Archer."

Will's eyes narrowed. "And you sir, will not allow it."

"Or else what?" his lordship growled.

"Or else we – Thea and I – will have nothing more to do with you."

His lordship snorted. "Think you've got everything going your way, now that you've got a bit of property to draw on? You're still only the heir, and you'd better not forget your place."

Will looked at Thea for a long moment, and the world seemed to hang in the balance. She didn't think he would surrender, exactly, but she – like Will – had come to know Lord Carrington well enough to take the cunning old man, and his threats, seriously. She had no idea what exactly his lordship might do, but she suspected he could make life quite unpleasant if he wished to.

After all the uncertainty, the relief Will felt just now must be overwhelming. As long as he stayed on good terms with his lordship – no matter what that required – he would have everything he wanted. She could hardly fault him for trying to keep the peace. It was his nature, as well as his profession, to find compromises.

"My place," Will said gently without taking his gaze off her, "is beside my wife. If it comes to cutting ties, my lord, we won't want anything of yours. Not your money, or the family estate, or the jewelry." He paused. "Or the title."

She couldn't stop herself. "Will!"

"See?" Lord Carrington snorted. "At least the girl has a little sense."

Thea ignored him. "Will? You would do that?"

"Yes. If that's what you want."

183

She couldn't even speak.

"It turns out that after all that fuss, I don't care about any of it," Will said. "Not as much as I care about you. So if you don't want to put up with all this aggravation, Thea, we'll turn it down. We'll give it all back."

"But – but this is why you married me, Will. And now you're the heir again."

"I was a fool to think all of that mattered, when I have the greatest treasure already. I have you." He reached out to cup her cheek. "I know I said marriage wasn't my first choice – but as it turns out, you are the only woman I can imagine being married to. It's really only been a short while since we met. But what we've been through together in those few days... I've learned how special you are. How perfect you are for me. Thea – I've fallen in love with you."

Her throat closed up, and tears threatened to blind her. She shook her head a little.

Will sighed. "I shouldn't have said it. Put it down to the confusion and all the emotional upset. I know you don't feel the same. Maybe someday you might... but for now, please just forget I said anything. Let me just treasure you as my wife."

"I can't forget it," she whispered. "Because I love you too."

He caught her tightly in his arms, and she didn't mind that they were still standing at the edge of Grosvenor Square, surrounded by a fascinated crowd, as he kissed her till her head spun.

Lady Carrington sniffed. "How perfectly vulgar – and how utterly predictable."

His lordship glared at her. "We all make mistakes, Penelope. I won't throw your foolishness in your face, if you'll let my past indiscretions lie. It isn't Thea's fault."

Will broke off their kiss, and Thea turned her head to make sure she was hearing correctly.

Lady Carrington held firm for a moment. Then she nodded once, stiffly.

His lordship put a hand on the small of his wife's back and turned her toward the house. Then he paused and said over his shoulder, "About that offer I made, Archer. It still stands. Five thousand guineas if there's a baby on the way by the end of the first year. Ten if it's a boy."

"Lord Carrington." Will pulled Thea back into his arms. "Go to the devil."

And the crowd started to applaud.

Epilogue

Five Years Later

Will drew in a long, deep breath full of the scents of closely-mown grass and roses heavy on the bush, and smiled contentedly down at his wife.

"Summer at Tanner's Close is the very best time of all," Thea said.

"It's nice. But I'm partial to Christmas."

"That's because you're really only a big child at heart."

"No, it's because snuggling under a pile of blankets is so much fun."

"And sneaking away on a summer afternoon isn't?"

"Are you suggesting we try it?" He tipped his head toward a group on the lawn. "They all seem to be absorbed, and if you keep looking at me like that..."

Thea smacked his arm. "Do you have nothing else to think about?"

"It's not entirely my fault, Thea. His lordship seems to believe it's time for our third."

"And every time he drops a hint, you send him a perfectly massive bill for his legal work."

"Which he ignores."

"Still, I'd think by now he'd have made the connection." A raised voice from the lawn drew Thea's attention. "We'd better go see what's going on there."

"I'm fairly sure my mother can keep the rest of them in line." He reached for her hand as they strolled nearer.

A little girl knelt on a blanket spread on the grass, pouring pretend tea for a row of dolls and for one very large male who had folded himself up to sit beside her. "That one fell over," she pointed out. "Pick it up."

The man reached out to straighten the doll.

From her chair nearby, Lady Carrington sniffed. "You are spoiling that child."

A little boy looked up from a set of wooden blocks he was stacking into some sort of castle and said to the woman who was helping him, "Grandmama Archer, you always say fruit is spoiled when it smells funny. But Annabel doesn't smell funny. Much."

"*You* smell, Giles," Annabel retorted.

"Enough," Thea said. "Annabel, you seem to have forgotten to say *please*."

"Yes, Mama." The child fixed her gaze on Lord Carrington and displayed a dimpled smile. "Please, *please*, sir, will you pick up my dolly? And thank you for doing it already."

Will, who had been on the receiving end of that melting gaze too many times himself – for Annabel had inherited Thea's big brown eyes – felt a flash of sympathy for his daughter's victim.

Not that Lord Carrington seemed to mind, for he chuckled – chuckled! – and stretched out a hand. "Help me up, Archer." Will clasped his lordship's arm and pulled him to his feet. "Good thing you came along. If I'd sat on that hard ground any longer I'd never move again."

Annabel looked thoughtful for a moment, and then she turned her smile on Lady Carrington. "Please, ma'am. Grandmama Archer is playing with Giles, so will you play dollies with me?"

"Certainly not, child." But there was no heat in her ladyship's tone, and she added, "I will, however, read to both you and Giles if Nurse brought out the book of fairy tales."

"The *whole* book?" Anna asked hopefully.

"Annabel," Thea warned.

"We'll see," her ladyship said.

"That means yes," Lord Carrington muttered. "She'll read till her voice gets hoarse. And she says *I'm* spoiling them? Walk with me, Archer. I want to talk to you. There's a factory I'm considering buying into, up north. A very lucrative possibility, but–"

"I assume there's a contract to review?"

"Of course. Think I'm a dolt? You know, my boy, I never thought I'd say it. But I do believe after all is said and done, the title will be safe in your hands."

"And with Thea, you mean. Of course."

"Funnily enough, I wasn't thinking of Thea just then. But since you've mentioned her..."

Will braced himself.

"The twins are almost four years old and it's past time to be thinking about a spare. Now about that investment..."

"I'll happily review the contract, sir," Will said cheerfully. "For a –" *very large* "fee."

"I would expect nothing less." Lord Carrington grinned and slung an arm around Will's shoulders as they crossed the lawn to the house.

About the Author

Leigh Michaels is the author of more than 100 books, including contemporary romance novels, historical romance novels, and non-fiction books including local history and books about writing. She is the author of *Writing the Romance Novel*, which has been called the definitive guide to writing romances.

Six of her books have been finalists in the Romance Writers of America RITA contest for best traditional romance of the year, and she has won two Reviewers' Choice awards from Romantic Times (RT Book Review) magazine. More than 35 million copies of her books have been published in 25 languages and 120 countries around the world. She teaches romance writing at Gotham Writers Workshop.

Other Books by Leigh Michaels

Regency-period historical romance

The Regency Scandals -- 4 book series

The Mistress' House #1

Number Five, Upper Seymour Street is the perfect love nest.

Tucked away in a discreet corner of London, it would be an ideal site to conduct affairs... except this elegant townhouse has a way of making its residents fall in love instead.

Anne — the perfect mistress for the rakish Earl of Hawthorne;

Felicity — the perfect challenge for Richard, Lord Colford;

and Georgiana — the perfect nightmare for Major Julian Hampton...

the residents of Number Five, Upper Seymour Street.

Just One Season in London #2

Meet the Ryecrofts...the family that courts together.

RYE – Viscount Ryecroft is a young man with a problem. Make that two problems: He has a beautiful sister to marry off – but no money to fund a London Season for her. Perhaps he needs to find an heiress for himself first?

SOPHIE – Miss Sophie Ryecroft is willing to marry for the good of the family – but since she can't meet the sort of man Rye has in mind for her except in London, she's looking for alternatives.

MIRANDA – Rye and Sophie's mother, the dowager (but still young) Lady Ryecroft, will do anything for the sake of her children – even taking up again with a man she knew long ago, and offering to be his mistress.

Only in London can the Ryecrofts find their destinies...

Find the full list
at leighmichaels.com

The Wedding Affair #3

The Duke of Somervale's sister is getting married in the wedding of the year – but the wedding guests are in the mood for affairs, not vows!

The Duke needs the help of beautiful, stubborn Olivia Reyne to fight off the debutantes who have taken over his country estate. Olivia's willing to help – at a price which will secure the future for her small daughter.

Penny Townsend sees the wedding as her last chance to salvage her arranged marriage and turn it into something more than a matter of convenience.

And vicar's daughter Kate Blakely needs a job – and fast – before she gives in to the tempting presence of her first love!

The Birthday Scandal #4

A Regency birthday party leads to love – and scandal!

When Lucien, Isabelle, and Emily are invited to their great-uncle's 70th birthday party, they hope the elderly duke's promise to make their lives easier means they'll be receiving cash. What they don't expect to find is love... and scandal!

Lucien, incensed by his father's announcement that he's marrying a girl even younger than Lucien, resolves to convince the bride to back out – no matter what it takes.

After a year of a marriage of convenience, Isabel is horrified to find her husband occupying the room next door – and making it clear he intends to move into her bed.

And Emily, disillusioned by the whole notion of marriage after the death of her fiancé, decides it's time to take a lover instead...

Three siblings, three romances – and three scandals — keep the *ton* buzzing in this Regency romp!

Gentleman in Waiting

Everything depends on the baby...

Lady Mariah Gerrard anxiously awaits the birth of her stepmother's child, hoping for a boy who will inherit their father's title so Mariah can gain access to her dowry and her freedom. Her father's cousin John, the next heir in line, has other plans – if the baby is a girl, disaster looms.

When Myles Moreton comes to Edgeworth to manage the family estate, Mariah's no longer certain that even the birth of a boy will solve her problems. Why is money missing? Why is Mariah's dowry in doubt? Despite his genial façade, is Cousin John planning mischief – or worse? Why is Myles Moreton, rather than the late earl's trustees, suddenly in control? And how can Myles – a man who's entirely ineligible – be not only completely maddening but utterly charming and very, *very* tempting?

As the family gathers to await the birth, Mariah and Myles search for answers – and they find that playing the waiting game can have its own rewards.

Ruining the Rake

A desperate young lady...

When Elinor's guardian arranges her marriage to an elderly merchant interested only in her society connections, she will do anything to sabotage the wedding – even if it means ruining herself by running off with another man.

A gentleman rake...

Who could be a better choice for a woman who needs ruining than Lord Rackham – a man so notorious that all of London calls him Lord Rake?

A straightforward bargain...

But when their arrangement goes awry, saving Elinor may mean ruining the rake!

Award-winning contemporary romance

The Lake Effect

When high-powered attorney Kane Forrestal abandons his career and takes up beach combing, his firm reacts by sending Alexandra Jacobi to talk him into coming back. Trouble is, who's going to end up persuading whom?

The Lake Effect was a finalist in the Romance Writers of America RITA contest for best sweet traditional romance of the year.

Traveling Man

When the host of the Kansas City Morning TV show has a heart attack, the station manager brings in traveling feature reporter Quinn Randolph to "help out" the co-host, Emily Lambert. But Quinn isn't exactly helping matters... he's flirting with Emily and taking over the show, and soon Emily's life feels like a disaster zone.

Traveling Man was a finalist in the Romance Writers of America RITA contest for best sweet traditional romance of the year.

Ties that Blind

It isn't that Abbey Stafford doesn't want her widowed mother to marry again; she just doesn't think Janice has made a good choice in Frank Granger, the neighborhood handyman. And Abbey isn't the only one to think so: Frank's son Flynn is just as opposed to the match— and to having Abbey in his life.

Until they team up to stop the wedding – and discover that they're far more interested in each other than in the older generation.

Ties that Blind was a finalist in the Romance Writers of America RITA contest for best sweet traditional romance of the year.

The Daddy Trap

Lindsay wanted a baby, Gibb didn't – and their marriage broke up over the disagreement. Now Gibb's back in town, and their attraction is just as strong. But Gibb still doesn't want a child – and Lindsay now has an eight-year-old son.

The Daddy Trap was a finalist in the Romance Writers of America RITA contest for best sweet traditional romance of the year.

Family Secrets

Chase Worthington might be a dropdead handsome hunk of movie star, but he doesn't know beans about raising his child – four-year-old Nicky's tantrums are all the evidence Amanda Bailey needs. Nicky goes through nannies at the speed of light – until Chase goes on location in the small town of Springhill, Iowa, and Amanda, the manager of the local inn, enters the scene.

Family Secrets received a Reviewer's Choice Award from Romantic Times (RT Book Reviews).

The Best-Made Plans

Penn Caldwell was the love of Kaitlyn Ross's youth, but he left town rather than make a commitment. So now that he's back, why is she having second thoughts about her engagement to another man?

Books for writers

Writing the Romance Novel

Award-winning romance novelist Leigh Michaels talks you through each stage of the writing and publishing process. From the origins and evolution of the romance novel to establishing a vital story framework to writing that last line to seeking out appropriate publishers, everything you ever wanted to know about writing a romance novel is here in "the definitive guide to writing the romance novel."

Writing Between the Sexes

Men and women think, talk, and act differently – which causes problems for writers who are trying to create characters of the opposite sex. When we understand the difference between masculine and feminine qualities and habits, we can use those behaviors and patterns to create characters who are plausible and unique, but not stereotypical. *Writing Between the Sexes* will help you to identify your own gender-specific behaviors, notice those of the opposite sex, and use both to make your characters realistic and believable.

Non-fiction

Another Taste of Love

Practical recipes for the busy cook – from appetizers to desserts

For the Love of Tea

Whether it's a cup with a friend or an elegant afternoon affair, tea is a fun and flexible way to entertain. Leigh shares her favorite tea parties – including formal tea receptions, Mad Hatter's Tea Parties, picnic teas, happy hour teas, and more – complete with menus and recipes.

Much Ado About Shakespeare
*Who wrote the plays and poems
credited to William Shakespeare?*

Though professors and English teachers would have you believe the matter is settled and the author of *Hamlet* and *Romeo and Juliet* and *Much Ado about Nothing* has long since been identified, that is far from true.

There are good reasons to doubt that the man who was born and died in Stratford-upon-Avon was ever any kind of writer, much less the most honored author in the English language.

As time goes on, the number of doubters – including authors, actors, attorneys, doctors, judges, university professors, and scholars of English literature – continues to grow, as does the list of books documenting the many reasons for doubt.

MUCH ADO ABOUT SHAKESPEARE is a quick introduction to the authorship question. If you've heard that there's a squabble about who Shakespeare really was, but you don't know much about it – or if you've simply wondered what all the fuss is about – this 10,000-word summary is a good starting place.